M000048311

I am the mate and companion of people, all just as immortal and fathomless as myself,
(They do not know how immortal, but I know.)

Every kind for itself and its own, for me mine male and female,
For me those that have been boys and that love women,
For me the man that is proud and feels how it stings to be slighted,
For me the sweet-heart and the old maid, for me mothers and the mothers of mothers,

For me lips that have smiled, eyes that have shed tears,
For me children and the begetters of children.

-**Walt Whitman,** *from Song of Myself, Leaves of Grass*

[handwritten: Belinda, Buon Natale, Michael Pedretti]

MICHAEL PEDRETTI

Begetters
of
Children

Book III of a 12 part series titled

The Story of Our Stories

Busting Boundaries, Williamsburg, VA

Print ISBN: 978-1-54397-436-2

eBook ISBN: 978-1-54397-437-9

CONTENTS

Preface..ix

Introduction..xi

Part I...3

Part II...33

Addenda..61

    Ahnentafel Chart for Stefano Maria Pedretti.....................63

    San Bernardo..73

    Pedigree Chart...119

    Primary Documents..121

    The Heroic Epic: an Essay..172

Preface

You and I, we are cousins – we are of the genes of Mitochondrial Eve and we share the same genes of tens of billions of Eve's children. It is possible that as many as 115 billion people were born before us. But you and I have each had more than one hundred billion ancestors since the first settlers arrived on the eastern side of the Mount of San Bernardo overlooking the Valley of San Giacomo in Sondrio, Lombardy, Italy around 700 AD.. If you trace our ancestry back to the time of Caesar each of us would have to identify more than 288 quadrillion grandparents or 288 million billion ancestors. If you would like to fill out your family chart dating back to the mythological Eve born around 4,004 BC, you would have to identify seven times as many people or 1.6 to the 57th power. What if we go back to the year of the first Eve? Let's not even go there.

Sorry, I got lost in the numbers. You get the idea. There is no way, with that many ancestors, that you and I do not share a few billion of the same grandparents, making us not double cousins, not even cousins tens of thousands of times, but cousins more than a billion times over. Our genes are so intertwined we are closer than brothers, closer than sisters, maybe even closer than twins.

This story will tell you a story of how things are, of how things were, of who we are and were and will be; you and me.

This is not just the story of Peter and Adelaide Pedretti, not just the story of Tom and Mary Venner, it is about us. This story is our story. These tales are as much your tales as they are mine. We have lived it together, we are living it together, we will live it together. You and I; we are not only twins; we are joined at the heart. To quote Walt Whitman, "Every atom belonging to me as good belongs to you."

Introduction

"I sing of arms and man"

-Virgil, *The Aeneid*

"I sing of kindness and woman"

-Pedretti, *The Story of Our Stories*

The mandate for an epic is to identify and celebrate who the people are and what their potential is. In Homer and Virgil's times the epic hero was a male warrior, whose violent behavior led to victories that inspired loyalty, patriotism and submission to the ruling class. "I sing of arms and man," is the opening line of Virgil's poem about a brutal warrior who begets a bellicose Rome and the ancestors of combatant Caesar Augustus. His epic celebrated empire builders, encouraged retaliation and downplayed the massive cost of lives, enforced slavery and legalized classism.

Should the modern epic celebrate dominance, war and revenge? Will today's epic promote limitation, exclusion and restriction? Is it not possible to put the historic, gentry- sponsored classism, war, violence, and tribalism into the past? Isn't today's hero the commoner, making things happen by mass commitment rather than individual supremacy—more interested in planting seeds than in accumulating power, in making advancements rather than blowing up people, tradition, and peace - more willing to fight for fair treatment with words than domination by war-- more concerned with kindness than control--capable of letting empathy replace revenge?

Today's epic hero is a planter – one who plants and cultivates; one who plans and nourishes. Our hero has no power or desire to raid the work of others. Our hero cannot come from the privileged class, by definition a people who rely on other's plantings to harvest their successes. Our story is not the story - cannot be the story - of someone indulging in the unjust wealth born of another's labor. No, our story is hidden in the mothers, "Who long since left the shores of craving, supremacy and war to explore generosity, affection and creativity."

Come; join me in play, kindness and song.

> I sing of kindness and of woman
> Serf no more, never Lord
> And of the suffering they endured
> Trodden under the might of the Sons of Misogyny
> Those ministers of misery who maltreated our mothers
> Turning brother against sister, husband against wife,
> Parent against child, mother against mother.
> Tell me, reader, how it all began, why so much spite?
> What did our mothers do to deserve their vengeance?

In the Aeneid, Virgil celebrated the Roman conqueror; I celebrate the planter of seeds. Virgil celebrated war; I celebrate harmony. Virgil celebrated dominance; I celebrate parity. Virgil praised father Augustus; I praise mother Eve.

The Story of our Stories is the story of Peter and John, of Adelaide and Stefano, and Marianna and Petronella, about Agnes and her children. It is about the individuals who peopled the Mount of San Bernardo and who turned the roughness of Bad Ax into the gentleness of Genoa, but first and foremost it is our story, the story of you and me. Our story is written as an epic composed of 12 books each with a supportive addendum. Each book covers a different story, some covering the life of a typical family member of a specific generation, others reflecting many people of a generation, another tracing the entire story from beginning to now and one looking into a future predicated by the behavior of our mothers. Each volume tells a critical part of the story, is an integral part of the whole and plays into the unfolding of the epic. While arranged by number, each book can be read independent of the rest.

THE STORY OF OUR STORIES

Titles of the 12 Volumes

I. Time to Journey Home

II. The Veneid

III. Begetters of Children

IV. Lost Book of Prima Maria Della Morte

V. L'ultima Preghiera

VI. Lettere d'Amore

VII. John

VIII. Peter, the Biography

IX. Book of Agnes

X. Hoe-ers

XI. Mick: the Memoirs of a Planter

XII. Il Lavoro di Artisti

THE STORY OF OUR STORIES

BOOK III

Begetters of Children

"This story I want to tell you about how things are.
This story I want to tell you about how things were.
This story I want to tell you about how things will be."
                                        –Walt Whitman

(In this book, I tell yarns made from fabricated woofs being woven through the warp of fact making a tapestry that captures the truth. You could unravel the fabrications from the facts that so often warp the truth, but in the process, you may also unravel the record of meaning).

Part I

"Here we will be safe from war, pestilence and thievery," Nico explained to his seventeen followers, after leading them to a god-forsaken spot high up in the Alpine mountains in an uncivilized area located in neither Italy nor Switzerland. Nico's Seventeen had barely escaped the ravages of the war between Louis II, the son of King Charles the Bald, and the Vikings. This group of migrators had witnessed their wives and sisters raped by the Vikings when they conquered their village just off the Po River. They were elated when Louis' soldiers pushed out the Vikings, but in days, Louis' Liberators became known as Louis' Liquidators as his soldiers killed their parents, children, and friends and then devoured their food. Those who survived began to die of the fever bought to their village by both camps. When Nico had offered to lead the survivors out of this hell, they did not hesitate to follow him even though they did not know him, and had no reason to trust him. Nico had fought in Louis' army. Disgusted with his fellow soldiers' behavior, he decided to escape and to take the survivors of the village with him. He had them gather what seeds they had, cage their chickens and rabbits and gather their goats in order to leave as soon as dark would cover their escape.

After days of hiding by day and traveling by night, all but starving and living constantly in fear of both the soldiers and the people whose land they were trespassing, they had come onto a valley that reminded them of their village where their ancestors had lived off the fertile land for longer than any story stretched. Feeling safe here from the enemy, they set up camp. Some thought as they fell asleep that night, "Here we can rebuild our Eden."

The next morning, Nico ordered everyone to pack up and head straight up the forbidding mountain. After weaving back and forth in order to get ever higher, they came upon a small clearing. Nico continued, "This is where we will settle. We will clear the land, use the timber to build houses and stables and call this mountainside our home." As the Seventeen stood in the small opening surrounded by trees and brush many regretted they had trusted this stranger. The next day Nico instructed his two sons, boys of seven and nine, to take the group's nine goats to graze higher on the mountain. Thus began the time-honored tradition of taking the livestock high in the mountain to graze during the summer months so that the grain and grass growing in the cleared fields could be harvested for winter feed for their livestock. In the small clearing where they settled, the women and girls set up a home for the rabbits and chickens that would provide the main subsistence for the group. On the far side of the open space, they planted seven saplings they prayed would grow into apple trees, along with four short rows of grape vine cuttings they had safeguarded on their journey. Under Nico's leadership, the seven adult males began to fell the trees, strip them of their branches for firewood for the winter, and lay out the trunks to make walls for their new homes. As they cleared the land, they laid stones along the lower edge and scraped top soil from the forest bed just above the clearing to cover the area with 3 inches of rich soil. The wives planted cabbage, rhubarb, turnips, mint, peas, chard, spinach, celery, parsnip, curled parsley, radish and ground cherries. At the same time, the husbands prepared the land to receive the seeds they had hoarded to grow short oat, bristle-pointed oat, and alfalfa to be able to feed their animals through the winter. The women gathered berries, mushrooms, currants, and gooseberries to feed the settlement that first summer, thereby allowing the number of rabbits and chickens to multiply so they could be eaten during the winter. In the fall, the children were sent out to collect bags full of chestnuts. The men continued to clear the forest so they would have more tillable land the next summer. They gathered rocks from above the place where they would build homes and rolled them into their new village to form a base for their timbers. Before the first snowstorm, they had built two houses and three stables to protect the people and their animals from the fierce mountain winter.

The new citizens of what would someday be known as San Bernardo frazione di San Giacomo Filippo, located in the province of Sondrio in Lombardy, Italy got through the first winter without butchering even one goat as they knew they had to build the herd for future winters. As their supplies of chestnuts, chickens, rabbits, and apples were dwindling, the snows began to melt and the goats gave birth. The children and women milked the dams providing milk and cheese, which lasted until the early crops came in.

Nico knew his wife Fabrina and she bore Umberto who, during his twelfth year, cleared, on a bet, one entire acre of forest. Then as a personal goal, cleared two hundred square yards of forest each year from his thirteenth birthday until the year he died, allowing him to pass onto his son, Nico, the third largest farm on the mountain. To Nico, the son of Umberto, was born Giovanni, and Giovanni begat Laurentii who begat Josep. When Josep lived for 32 years, he left the mountain to work for a farmer who raised sheep as well as chickens, rabbits and goats. There Josep took Pia as his wife and they begot Jozef. After the birth of Jozef, Josep returned to his home and brought with him six sheep, the first to graze on San Bernardo Mountain. Under Josep's watchful eye the sheep multiplied and Josep traded his sheep for chickens, rabbits and goats. Josep taught the men of San Bernardo how to shear the sheep and Pia taught the women how to turn the wool into thread and cloth. Soon Josep was the wealthiest man on the mountain and he employed several of his young cousins to loosen and shape the schist found just outside their village into flat stones. He layered and cemented the stone with a formula of clay and schist dust wetted by a mixture of liquids he had learned about while living in the valley, to form the walls of the house he built for Pia. This was the first stone house built in San Bernardo. The people saw the value of stone for their houses and from that day forward, when a new family needed a home or one of the timber houses burned or rotted out, the owners built their homes with stone. When Josep had completed his house, he begat Guglielmo, Giovanni and Giacomo. Giacomo begat Filippo who fought in the cavalry for the House of Savory, helping them to establish dominance over all of northern Italy.

This is the record of Filippo's line, who begat Jozef who begat Marcello who formed a regiment of boys from Olmo, San Bernardo and Sommarovina to push back the soldiers of Henry V who had come to steal the harvest and ravage the woman of San Bernardo. When Marcello had lived 54 years, he begat Anna Maria. After he begat Anna Maria he lived 49 years and begat sons and daughters. Marcello lived 103 years, long enough to see Anna Maria inspire the people of the mountain of San Bernardo to build a church. In 1189 the Bishop of Como consecrated the San Bernardo Church as a holy space where the citizens of San Bernardo and the surrounding communities could worship, become baptized, wed and be buried. In order to feed the workers who came from Chiavenna to build the church, Anna introduced cows for the first time. At first, the men of San Bernardo laughed at Anna saying the land was too barren to feed cows, as they were much bigger eaters than the sheep, goats, rabbits and chickens they raised. Anna used the meat and the milk of the cows to feed the workers who had come to build the church and the people of San Bernardo saw that the cows were good and from that time each family kept two or three cows in their stables.

Anna Maria begat Francesco, Teresa and Domenica who married a man from Vho. When Domenica's great grandson and his wife were the only humans in Vho to survive the Black Plague that ravished the valley in 1348, they became known as the survivors and when they gave birth to Michele, he was called by all Michele Della Morte – Michael who came from death. Michele is the ancestor of all Della Mortes who have multiplied and spread over the earth.

Francesco and his wife Domenica begat one child, Guglielma Maria who worshiped every day in the San Bernardo church and became known as the Maria Magdalene of San Bernardo. The people of San Bernardo honored their saintly Magdalene with a variety of pet names such as Mag, Dalene, and Gdalene. Over time, Gdalene became Gadalene that became Gadolene that became Gadola. Guglielma and her husband conceived a son who was given the name Salvatore M'Godala to honor his mother, and his offspring became known as of the Gadola house. Salvatore begat Guglielmo who called his daughter Guglielma who called her son Guglielmo and for the next four generations the family living in the house of Gadola called their eldest son Guglielmo.

The second son of the fourth Guglielmo was Victori. Whatever Victori planted died; it was said he did not have a green thumb. On the other hand, Victori was gifted with the knife and was sent to apprentice with his uncle who owned a meat shop in Chiavenna. Victori became known for his ability to carve the exact amount of meat in the manner wanted to make the perfect meal. Upon returning to the mountain of San Bernardo, Victori, who was already known as The Butcher, established the first butcher shop in the village where the farmers traded their harvests for his services. One of Victori's special recipes was to slice thin strips of cow meat, soak them overnight in a salt solution and spread them out on the sun to dry. Farmers from Olmo and even from the valley would bring their meat to Victori to prepare it. After forty years of curing beef in his manner, Victoria accidently knocked a slab of meat into the brine before he had sliced it into dryable pieces. As he reached to pull the prime cut of meat from the brine, he twisted his back and was bed ridden for nineteen days and nineteen nights. Victori's apprentice carried on the butchering for the village to the best of his ability. When Victori returned there was much to do to catch up. After eleven more days, Victori was ready to make some more of his famous dried beef. However, in his pail of brine was the slab he had forgotten about. He reached into the pail and scooped out the slab. He noticed that the outside of the meat had contracted and built a protective coat. As he was about to ask his apprentice to dispose of the meat, he brought the slab up to his nose to smell it. It did not smell rotten. Meat a whole month old that had never been dried ought to stink. He asked himself, "Could I set the entire piece in the sun to let it cure?" Then he answered himself, "No, I cannot put such a large piece in the sun; it will certainly rot." Still he was reluctant to throw it away or to cook or eat it. "I think I will hang it up near the back door and wait for it to prove it is rotten." The back corner of his shop was always shaded and there was a gentle breeze coming through the two windows that The Butcher always kept open to keep his shop smelling fresh. Each day, Victori would put his nose up to the meat, and each day he would discover that it did not stink. He did notice that it began to dry and look similar to the thin strips of meat that he cured in the sun. After twenty-one more days, Victori took down the meat, rolled it in his hands, squeezed it, smelled it and thought. "It cannot be rotten. I will try a tiny piece. It cannot kill me." Victori sliced the tiniest sliver of meat off the slab and put it to his mouth. He held it in his mouth, testing for the taste of bad meat. Instead, he found the meat to be most delicious. "I will wait until tomorrow to see if it makes me sick." But he could not wait. He sliced another slice as thin as possible and ate it. Then another piece. And so the day went with Victori slicing the thinnest slice his skilled hands could make. When he woke the next morning, he was not sick. "The meat cannot be bad." He said aloud. That day he sliced more – always the thinnest possible piece because he was still afraid it might be bad and it might kill him. His apprentice asked for a piece and Victori again sliced a thin piece. The apprentice asked for more. That night he told everyone in the village that Victori was keeping for himself the best tasting meat ever known to man. The next morning, when he opened his butcher shop, Victori found the entire village waiting to taste his meat. Victori had to slice the remaining slab in even thinner slices so everyone could have a taste. All agreed it was the sweetest, most tender, tasty piece of meat and that fall, when the farmers brought their cow to Victori to butcher, every one of them asked Victori to make several slabs of meat like the one he had served them that morning.

Victori, a little tired of people asking him to prepare that meat he accidently made by wrenching his back, decided he should give a name to the meat he soaked in brine for 30 days and hung in the cool air for 19 days. Since the meat was left to "stew" in brine for 30 days and 30 nights, Victori decided to call it bresada as in that which has stewed or braised. When Victori told Paola, his wife, of his new name, she laughed and said your invention is not cooked, how can you call it braised? "Si, Si. But I need a name. And it does "stew" in the brine."

Paola and Victori thought about what to name the sweet meat. That night Paola had a dream about Victori calling her "Sweet" which was his favorite nickname for her while offering her a taste of the "sweet" meat braised in the stew of salt and water. She woke up saying bresweet, sweetbre, sweetpaola, brepaola, bresaola. Victori liked mixing stewed with sweet and using his sweet Paola's name instead of sweet and so to this day the accidental discovery of Victori is called bresaola.

This is the line of the fifth Guglielmo who knew his wife and begat Guglielmo, Pietro, Bernardus, Guglielma, Anna, Teresa, Giorgio, Domenica, Magdalena, Alberto, Pia, Pina, and Marianna. None of Guglielmo's children lived to get married except Pietro, who begat Guglielmo in the year of 1502.

When Pietro's son was born, he was baptized with the name of Guglielmo to honor the father of his father who was from the house of Gadola. In a certified and notarized ceremony, on the sixth day of October in the year one thousand, five hundred and fifty three Guglielmo was granted, by the Duke of Milan, the right to acquire a new surname. The deed of courage committed by Guglielmo that led to this honor has been lost in history. Wanting to honor his father, he took the name of Pedretto, which means the son of Pedro. In the dialect of Valle San Giacomo, Pietro was pronounced Pedro; hence, the son became Pedretto and not Pietretto.

The Gadola family were leaders of the mountain town of San Bernardo, a part of the independent territory of Valle San Giacomo, located in the land between the Swiss to the North and the Italians of Chiavenna to the south. The Gadola family is reputed to have maintained detailed records of the exploits of their family. While these records were destroyed by the soldiers of Napoleon in 1806, the story is still told of how the precursors of the Gadola family arrived in San Bernardo shortly after the turn of the twelfth century. The family cleared away three acres of land about 5000 feet above the settlement where the church had been built and they called their new sub-division Scannabecco. The family was industrious and continued to clear additional land building Scannabecco into the largest sub-division of San Bernardo. By the generation of Pietro, the Gadola house was the most respected in San Bernardo. Pietro Gadola owned three cows, five goats and seven lambs. This livestock produced more food than Pietro's family could use, so each fall he drove some down the mountain to trade for rice, spices from the Far East, and wine and cheeses from Milan. It was on one of these trips that Pietro was introduced to a new fruit that was juicy, red and grew on vines. He was told the fruit had been bought back from the new world by the British and introduced to the Milan area the previous year. Pietro found the fruit to be of his liking. The next spring, Pietro drove his burro to the valley and purchased several seedlings of the plant called tomato by the local farm goods storeowner. Pietro found the plant to grow well on the mountain and shared its fruit with his neighbors. The tomato became the most productive fruit grown in San Bernardo gardens.

Guglielmo Pedretto, the eldest son of Pietro of the Gadola House, took Margherita the daughter of Francesco Michele Della Morte and Orsola Lombardini for his lawfully wedded wife and they begat nine children. They named their first son Pietro to honor Guglielmo's father, his second son Francesco to honor Margherita's father and their twins they called Giovanni and Guglielmo. Guglielmo and Margherita's first daughter was named Caterina to honor Guglielmo's mother. Before she reached the age of two, she died of the fever along with her baby sister Orsola. Guglielmo and Margherita named their third daughter Caterina who later married her first cousin Lorenzo Di Stefano, and lived and died in Olmo. There is no record that they ever birthed a child. Nine years after Caterina was born, Margherita gave birth to her second pair of twins who were baptized with the names of Petri and Petro, in the forty-eighth year of Guglielmo's life.

The eldest sons, Pietro and Francesco, were conscripted to fight in the war over the Duchy of Milan on behalf of the French King Francis I against the King of England. In the

bloody battle of Ceresole[1], which took place on the eleventh day
of April in the year 1544 outside the village of Ceresole d'Alba
in the Piedmont region of Italy, a Pikeman mercenary fighting
for the Spanish-Imperial army[Spain and England were allies]
of Alfonso d'Avalos d'Aquino, Marquis del Vasto, pierced Pietro
in the groin and then clubbed him to death. Giovanni, wanting to avenge the death of his older brother, joined the Italian
mercenary army fighting in the French service, under François
de Bourbon, Count of Enghien. His ferocious battle manner
called upon him the attention of the Count who put Giovanni
in charge of the sixth column. After the Battle of Serravalle in
June 1544 bought the war in Italy to an end, Giovanni returned
to San Bernardo, the mountain town of his birth.

Francesco also returned to the Mountain of San Bernardo.
After a particularly violent bout with grappa, his father dis-
inherited his eldest living son and cast him out of the house.
Francesco built a tiny shack, barely large enough to lie down
in, one-half kilometer up the mountain. Some said he hunted
there for many years, others thought he froze to death that first
winter. No one ever saw him again, although a whole generation of children in the village claimed they had seen "The
Angel Devil" from time to time sneaking about the village.
Some even claimed he threatened to kill them.

Guglielmo, who had stayed home to assist his aging
father, married Teresa, the only child of Stefano Falcinella, and
inherited the Falcinella property upon the death of his father-
in-law. Both Giovanni and Guglielmo were prosperous, clearing one acre of new land just up from Olmo and increasing
their herds by three. Giovanni, a war hero, was perceived to

---

1 Historian Bert Hall characterized this battle as "marvelously confused" Hall, *Weapons and Warfare*, 187.

have gained worldly knowledge and was elected and reelected to represent San Bernardo on the Consul of Val San Giacomo. In the Winter of The Great Snows, the year that Elizabeth of the Tudor House ascended to the throne in England, a mud slide rushed down the mountain smashing a half dozen homes in the upper most section of Scannabecco including the home of Giovanni Pedretto. Guglielmo led the town into rescuing his brother along with every one of the 12 people who otherwise would have been buried alive. However, the slide would have its toll for Anna, the wife of Francesco Gadola, was seriously wounded and did not survive childbirth. Guglielmo had been crushed when Giovanni's house had collapsed just moments after the rescuers had freed him from the rubble. Guglielmo suffered several broken ribs, two broken arms and a broken leg. He was on his way to recovering, but on December 26 took to bed with a fever and rattling cough. Six days later, he expired. On January 23, 1559, Filippo fu Piero Strozzi under whom Giovanni had fought journeyed to San Bernardo to bestow the "Highest Standard Status," the most prestigious award given to a commoner, upon Giovanni for his courageous role in the battle of Serravalle. When Filippo Strozzi was told that Giovanni's brother Guglielmo had sacrificed his own life to save the lives of 12 villagers, he accepted Giovanni's request that his brother be awarded the same honor posthumously.

Giovanni lived for 97 years and be begot twelve children with his wife Agnese Gadola, who was of the other Gadola house. In Giovanni's thirty-ninth year, Agnese begot their first child whom they named Guglielmo. Eleven months later, in the year that Pius V became the 225th leader of the religion of the people of San Bernardo, they gave birth to their second child whom they named Antonio to honor the life of Agnese's father who had died the previous year. Their third son, Giovanni, was elected in 1637 to serve on the consul of Val San Giacomo as the representative from all the villages of the San Bernardo Mountain. Among his responsibilities was to take a census of the population of San Bernardo in 1640. He reported that there were 153 people, 41 families, 46 homes of which 42 had stables, 72 cows, 619 sheep, 213 goats and that he was unable to count the chickens and rabbits. Giovanni sat in on all council meetings and was reputed to be merciless on debtors. At one time he had the council approve interest rates as high as 7% and strictly enforced the laws of imprisonments for debtors who failed to meet their obligations. He was rewarded for his diligence by being chosen by the members of the council to be the Ministrali in 1659 and was known for his fair if somewhat excessive, demands for retribution from citizens who violated the rules of the community.

Giovanni's younger sister, the eldest daughter of Agnese Gadola-Pedretto never came back from berry picking when she was five. His brother, Lorenzo went to work for a lumber baron in the valley. He never married, to the best knowledge of the citizens of San Bernardo, but they heard he lived a long life. Two boys and one of the girls were caught in a San Bernardo snowstorm and their bones were not found until spring. The youngest sister, Teresa, married Walter Buzetti, the brother of Pastor Lorenzo Buzetti and moved into his family's home in Lirone where they were blessed with 15 children and all but two survived their parents.

Teresa gave birth to Flora. A restless child, Flora traveled so far north she was on the other side of Switzerland. There she had, for the first time, a food that had come from the new country. It was white, grew in the ground like a carrot, and had little flavor of its own. Nevertheless, the people that Flora was visiting served this new food two and sometimes three times a day. They served it with chicken, pork, beef, and venison. They served it with vegetables. They seemed to serve it with everything. Flora discovered, as her hosts had some years earlier, this pasty food made a filling and delicious supplement. They told Flora that British settlers had brought the tuber back from their trips to America, where it was called a potato. They informed her that this tuber multiplied itself several times even in the short summer season of the mountain and that a harvest could last, if stored in a root cellar, until next summer's crop came in. Flora asked for and was given a sack full of the tubers and she headed back to Val San Giacomo to tell her family of this miracle food that grew under harsh circumstances and seemed indestructible. She planted half her sack in Lirone and hauled the other half to her grandfather and grandmother on the mountain. Agnese, with the help of her children, planted all of the tubers, careful to make sure that the eyes faced toward the sky before burying them. Each eye produced six or more young that each grew in size enough to feed even a hungry man. At harvest time, Agnese took two of the tubers, which in her native tongue were called "di patate," from each hill and put them aside to plant the next season. She then stored the remainder in the cellar where they kept bresaola, cheeses and special sausages made at butcher time. On winter solstice, Agnese realized that she had more potatoes than she and her family could eat and she bagged some up and went to the other families in the village telling them about the magical plant, explaining how to store and prepare them for meals. The people saw the value of the potato and each saved some to plant the next spring. In this manner, the potato came to San Bernardo, making the land more productive and allowing the town to grow. By the next census, the notary recorded that the population of San Bernardo had grown to 239 people, although the population of the rabbits, cows and sheep had remained about the same.

In the year of 1616, Giovanni's descendants gathered to celebrate his 90th year on earth. To honor Guglielmo's yield, the family changed their name from Pedretto [son of Pedro] to its current version of Pedretti [children of Pedro]. An unknown descendent created the family crest for the celebration. He divided the coat of arms into daylight and nighttime. In the lower two-thirds the artist showed a castle basking in pure red sunlight built on the boulders of Mt. San Bernardo, the castle representing that each member of the family was 'king" of his own home even if that home was built on barren rock. The upper third of the crest was painted in blue representing the 1/3 of the day we sleep. The ship of life sailing downwind, - its spinnaker filled with the breath of a greater being - between two stars [birth and death?] shining brightly on a calm sea with nary a cloud in the sky nor enemy ship in sight.

This is the record of Agnes and Giovanni's son Antonio's line. Antonio moved into his grandfather Guglielmo's house upon his death that took place during his 87th year on earth. Antonio married Valentina, the only child of Stefano De Stephano of the neighboring village of Olmo. Antonio and Valentina called their first-born Giovanni and begat three more children, all of them daughters. One married her maternal grandfather's neighbor and moved back to Olmo, her mother's village, one married Walter Buzetti's youngest brother, Carlo, and settled in Vho where they had one son they called Walter. The eldest daughter, Teresa, never married and became the housekeeper for Father Buzetti and later for Father Levi of Fraciscio. Upon the death of his wife's father Antonio became the owner of the Olmo property. When his older brother Guglielmo suddenly passed away with no heirs, Antonio also inherited his father's home, livestock and the sizable storage of goods his father had accumulated. Shortly after Valentina died in childbirth, Antonio wooed the most beautiful girl, some said most beautiful ever, from San Bernardo - Marianna, the daughter of Pietro and Anna Cerletti. Marianna could trace her family back to one of the young men who had come to Valle San Giacomo after surviving the slaughters following the failed uprising bought on by famine and the cruelty of the intruder soldiers against Charlemagne in 793. It is recorded in the church records that Antonio and Marianna, after begetting five girls, prayed and fasted for seven days and seven nights beseeching their God for a son. In Antonio's fifty-second year, Marianna gave birth to a spirited baby boy who was baptized Giovanni Pietro, in memory of his older half-brother who had died in a terrible accident involving a wild boar. They gave Giovanni a second name of Pietro in order to pay homage to Marianna's father in case they could have no more boys. After five more boys were born, Antonio was known to joke that his prayers had multiplied like the loaves.

Then disaster struck. In the year of one thousand, six hundred and twenty-nine the word reached San Bernardo that the people in the valley below them were being eaten alive by the fever, followed by news that the fever was indeed a sinister plague and had spread from Switzerland to Milan and beyond killing everything in sight. Antonio called the leaders of the community to plan for the inevitable day the fever would strike their community. Teresa, Antonio's eldest daughter with his first wife, proposed that the discussion move from what to do when the plague arrived to how to keep the plague at bay. At first, the members laughed at her naïveté, but there were some in the gathering who believed the new idea that the plague was passed from one person to another. If they could make it so no one living in San Bernardo had any contact with someone outside San Bernardo, they might be protected. So it was agreed that the citizens of San Bernardo would not be allowed to leave, and if they left they would not be allowed to return until the plague passed. The young men were ordered to build a barricade on the path to San Bernardo from Olmo in order to make that road impassible from either direction.

Few truly thought this would help. Antonio proposed that the villagers pray each day to San Rocco, the patron saint of dogs, who was believed to have powers to protect worshippers from sickness. The village leaders mandated that every man, woman and child of San Bernardo gather every morning at the church of San Bernardo to pray to San Rocco to protect them from the plague for that day. They pledged to San Rocco, if he protected their village from the plague, the parishioners would build a chapel in Scannabecco to venerate the good Saint. Three hundred and sixty five days later, when not one person of the mountain town of San Bernardo had suffered from the plague, the worshipers began to mine the mountainside for stones for the chapel. Over the next 1,327 days every parishioner from the very youngest to the very oldest, marched down to San Bernardo church and prayed to San Rocco to keep the plague away. Eight months after the plague had finished ravishing the populace living in the valley below San Bernardo, Antonio's cousin made his way up the mountain believing that San Bernardo had, like so many other communities, been completely wiped out by the plague. He worked his way around the wall of protection and walked to the village to find that everyone was there and that they had prospered during the plague. During the two plus years the plague ravished Northern Italy it had taken over 280,000 lives but not one citizen of San Bernardo. The citizens tore down that wall and used the timber and stone from the barricade to complete the new chapel in the heart of Scannabecco christening it San Rocco in honor of the saint who had miraculously kept the plague from them. In further homage to the Saint of good health and dogs, those who live in Scannabecco from that time on to this very day refer to their hamlet as San Rocco.

After the plague, Antonio and Marianna begat Teresa Rocco Maria Pietro, Rocco Maria, Silvestro, and Cristoforo, who was baptized in the newly completed chapel of San Rocco on sixth day of January of Antonio's seventy-fifth year on earth. Cristoforo went to work for a winery in Sondrio; Rocco married a woman from Gordona, the only daughter of Giovanni Mazzini. Upon Giovanni Mazzini's death, Rocco took over the Mazzini grocery store. Their offspring continue to live in Gordona to this day although one of their great grandsons, Giovanni Domenico the son of Giovanni Pedretti di Gordona relocated to Chiavenna in late 1744 and helped to populate that city with citizens bearing the family name. Silvestro, who married his second cousin Teresa, the daughter of Guglielmo Cerletti, inherited his grandfather's homestead and sired Guglielmo Maria, and Guglielmo Silvestro, Maria, Marianna and Stefano. There are no surviving records of what became of Pietro or the five older sisters.

After the plague of 1629, Giovanni Pietro, the elder son of Antonio Pedretti and Marianna Cerletti, showed no interest in farming. He used his inheritance to take over the Gadola tavern. Giovanni engaged his younger brothers to refurbish the property that his Uncle Primo Gadola had let run down over a lifetime of neglect. Giovanni, a boisterous and jolly owner, soon had a thriving business and the men of San Bernardo gathered once again at the Gadola Tavern, making it the center of activity for the village. However, not everyone was happy. Giacomo Gadola, the eldest son of Primo felt that his rightful inheritance had been pilfered. One Saturday evening in the year of 1637 Giacomo Gadola, after one drink too many, accused Giovanni Pietro Pedretti of making good on his back. Giovanni called Giacomo a worthless tit – Giacomo wished Giovanni a litter of mice be hatched in his brain – Giovanni responded with, "May you swallow a closed umbrella and excrete it open." Soon the two were punching each other out. Hauled before the magistrate of Val San Giacomo both were fined 42 lire each for disturbing the peace. Giovanni Pietro's blessed life would turn this scandal into another opportunity as Annamaria, the daughter of Ministrali Pietro Parachino, was charmed by the gall of the young man from the mountains and by and by they were married in Chiavenna's S. Lorenzo, the mother church of the Valley.

In the year after the marriage, with the help of his father-in-law, Giovanni waged a bitter campaign and won the seat for Consul from San Bernardo becoming the youngest council member in history. Giovanni joined the members of Central and North Val San Giacomo who wanted to create a government separate from Chiavenna. The council voted to collect taxes on behalf of Thomas in his siege on Milan. On December 4, 1639 after the surrender of Milan, Thomas the younger, brother of Victor Amadeus, in gratitude to the Council, decreed that Val San Giacomo's political structures would thereafter be independent from Chiavenna and that it would administer its own affairs by setting its own rates, electing its own justice administrators, and making its own political considerations. According to the *Archives of the Val San Giacomo Community 1538-1819* as translated by Carl Francoli:

> "The political and organisational administration of the Val San Giacomo was regulated according to their own customs. Their own communal regulations attested to a political life of great significance. The community of Val San Giacomo was divided into 12 quartieri, [quarters or wards] internally sub-divided into "squadre", or sub-localities, the overall valley being subdivided from 1650 into three regions called "terziere", the outer, the middle and the inner terziere.
>
> The outer terziere comprised the wards of St Giacomo, the mountains of San Bernardo, Olmo (or the mountains of both Olmo and Mezzo and Sommaravina) and Lirone.

The middle terziere comprised the wards of
    Campodolcino, Fraciscio, Starleggia, Portarezza
    and Vho.
The inner terziere comprised the wards of Isola,
    Pianazzo with Madesimo, and the remaining
    wards of Teggiate and Rasdeglia.
Thus the valley maintained the structure of a republic
    community by having three regions or "terziere",
    divided into four wards or "quartiere", which sub-
    divided into "squadre."

Shortly after being rewarded their independence, Giovanni Pietro, as an appointed assistant to the court of Val San Giacomo, took the leadership role in identifying and exterminating witches. He created the office of Deputy Against Crimes of Evil Spells and Witchcraft, and then appointed himself Deputy Chief. In 1646, he convinced the courts to find Maria Sciania guilty of witchcraft and to sentence her to hanging until dead. Many thought it was inevitable that he would be chosen as the next Ministrali of the Valley, but the honor would escape him his entire life. Giovanni continued to be a devoted witch hunter keeping the valley safe for the women and children who worshiped in the rightful church. Some thought Giovanni might soften his pursuit when his cousin Anna, the daughter of the late Andrea Gadola of San Giacomo, was accused of witchcraft based on the accusation of her daughter that she had failed to go to mass on the holy day of the Ascension of Mary into heaven. Anna claimed she had been bed ridden and both her doctor and priest testified at the trial that she had indeed been too ill to attend mass and to plead on her behalf. Nevertheless, the court, led by the righteous

Ministrali Francolo de Francoli and supported by the damning testimony of Giovanni Pietro Pedretti would hear nothing of that. They condemned Anna to perpetual exile from the Valley and the Church by beheading her in the courtyard of St. John the Baptist Church on March 28, 1657, burning her body on site and tossing her ashes in the Liro River to be carried away into oblivion. The people of the valley believed that only those whose bones remained intact would be resurrected at the second coming of their Lord. Burning her body and scattering the ashes of the notorious witch Anna Gadola would keep her from appearing at the second coming and prevent her from damaging their chances of meeting their maker in the end[2].

Giovanni Pietro and Annamaria begat four sons: Antonio, Pietro, Silvestro and Guglielmo. Antonio inherited his grandfather's farm and was content to spend his days farming, gossiping at the Gadola tavern and worshipping at the new San Rocco Chapel. He was known for telling his grandchildren that he never set foot off his beloved mountain after he returned at age 14 to work for and live with his grandfather.

Pietro, like his father and his maternal grandfather, became engaged in the politics of Val San Giacomo and at the early age of 36 became assistant Ministrali and, in the following year, took over the office everyone thought his father had earned but never attained. As Ministrali, Pietro oversaw the Valley through prosperity and famine. Near the end of the Great Drought of 1683, he authorized the city to pay for 40 masses to be said to plead for rain. When the rain came after

2 It is a fact that the Pedretti family dominated the politics of Val San Giacomo during the second half of the seventeenth century indicating that they had become a powerful family in their community. While there is no evidence yet that the dynasty of Giovanni, Pietro and Guglielmo Pedretti were in direct lineage to the Pedrettis descended from Stefano Pedretti, who immigrated to the USA in 1854, there is also no evidence that they were not. At the very least they were close relatives.

37 masses had been said, Pietro's position in the community was firmly established. For many years thereafter, Pietro and his baby brother Guglielmo alternated serving as Ministrali, but everyone knew that Guglielmo took his lead from Pietro.

When Guglielmo was thirty years old he wed Marianna Lombardini who had turned sixteen nine months earlier, and in 1653 they begat Giovanni, followed by Josep eleven months later. In the ninth year after giving birth to Josep and in her twenty-seventh year, Mariana again missed her period. Soon she was large with a baby who emerged on the twelfth day of January in the year 1664. The next day the newborn baby boy was christened Stefano. Marianna gave Guglielmo twelve more children over the next 14 years. After Josep, she gave birth to Stefano, and then Lorenzo, Teresa, Marianna, Orsola, Francesco, Maria, Caterina, Antonio, Battista, Giacomo, and Pietro Alberto. Guglielmo had to make two additions to his house to provide room for all of them to sleep, for his luck continued and not one of his children died before him.

Early in his life, Giovanni the eldest son of Guglielmo and Marianna showed a keen interest in the political life of his father and grandfather and honed his skills as an orator. The citizens of San Bernardo predicted a glorious future for their favorite son. However, the year after Pietro Alberto was born Giovanni was killed in a snow storm with his Uncle Silvestro. Crushed by the death of his grandson who was meant to carry on his name and his role in the community, Giovanni Pietro resigned as Ministrali, took to this bed and died within the year. Guglielmo also resigned from the council and retired to his home in Chiavenna where he devoted the rest of his years to gardening, painting and writing poetry. Josep became the rightful heir of the family property and took over the family farm. The rest of Guglielmo and Marianna's children, except for Orsola who became Father Monti's housekeeper, got married, moved off the mountain and had several children. Their descendants live in every region of Italy, Ticino in Switzerland, Paraguay, Australia, Canada, the United States and Venezuela.

San Bernardo eighteenth Century
San Rocco in background.

San Bernardo today

Vestige of early stone house

San Bernardo Church – 2010 – Photo by Luigi Fanetti

Hand painted crest hanging in Museum in Campodolcino

Painting of St. Rocco that hangs aside the altar in San Rocco

Part II

Devastated by the loss of his son and his eldest grandson, Giovanni Pietro Pedretti bequeathed the family farm to his oldest living grandson, Josep, who had never shown any interest in the political life of his father and grandfather and had spent his youth helping his Uncle Silvestro on the family farm. After losing his brother and uncle and inheriting the farm his uncle had operated, Josep showed more interest in grappa than farming. As Josep spent more and more time at the Gadola Tavern, his herd shrunk and his fields became more weed patches than oat fields. On a bitter cold February 6th with his sister Maria visiting to celebrate their mother Marianna's 69th birthday, Josep passed out on a two-meter high snowdrift on his way home. When 9 PM turned into 10 PM and her brother did not show, Maria was angry and concluded her good-for-nothing brother could not even give up his grappa and drunken friends to celebrate his mother's birthday. Marianna, always disappointed in her son, still believed in him enough to know he would not miss her birthday. Positive something was wrong and concerned that her son might be in trouble, she insisted Maria look for her brother. Maria left to go to the Gadola Tavern to drag her big brother home if necessary. Maria took her eldest son with her, but they found the tavern doors locked. Maria woke Giorgio Paiarola, the owner, and found out Josep had left nearly two hours earlier. The three called out for Josep as they walked back toward the house of Pedretti. As they were looking, a mountain blizzard blew in. Giorgio woke the nine other members of the San Bernardo

Rescue Squad to hunt for Josep, and his mother got on her knees and prayed to St. Joseph to save his namesake and to Saint Rocco to bring him home in good health. The odds of finding a drunk lost in a San Bernardo snowstorm were miniscule and odds of finding him alive were nil. Nevertheless, ten of the bravest villagers came together in the San Rocco church where they formed a flank bound together every two meters by whatever each rescuer had brought to tie themselves to their neighbor so that none of them would stray into death. In this manner, one of them stumbled across Josep who appeared to be frozen to death. They carried Josep back to the family home where his mother tended him back to life with prayer, blankets and love.

By the first thaw, his mother's magic led to a full recovery and thankful for the miracle of his life returned, Josep made his way to the San Rocco chapel, sunk to his knees and vowed never to touch a drop of grappa again. Two years later, he had recovered his grandfather's property and rebuilt the flock of sheep and goat herd back to what he had inherited. Deep in prayer one Sunday morning, he felt the presence of a woman next to his body. Not wanting to stare he turned just his eyes toward the warmth. He could make out a full flowing head of hair and a profile he found more than a little appealing. His heart fluttered for the first time in the presence of a woman. He wondered who she was. Was she from Chiavenna back for the day visiting her family? He told himself that he would turn to her at the end of services and he began to breathe deeper to build up the courage to talk to her. It would not be easy; he had not one female friend in the world. He had never dated, never wanted to date. Until that fateful night in the snow, grappa was his love and since then he had time only for Jesus, his farm and Saint Rocco. The mass trudged on for what seemed an eternity to Josep. He did not see the collection plate pass him or the priest turn bread and wine into the body and blood of Jesus. He even missed communion for the first time since finding the way. He smelled the sweetness of what stood next to him, felt the warmth, and he fell deeply in love. He asked himself, "How can I feel love when I don't even know who is next to me or what she even looks like for that matter?" Eventually, like all things, the mass was over and Josep had the opportunity to turn to his left and see who was next to him. For a split second, he saw not his neighbor but a vision, maybe even the Virgin Mary. There was a glow around her that said, "I am holy," a halo around her head that said, "I am sacred." But certainly, it was Uncle Giuseppe's daughter Margarita, the pig-tailed kid with freckles on her face he saw almost every day. Was it possible she was this stunning woman who had prayed next to him? Margarita said, "Hello", and turned to leave with her parents who sat in the pew across the aisle.

Josep tried hard to get her out of his mind, but he could not. She was young; too young for him. He did not even know how young, so he asked his mother if she knew how old she was. Fourteen. Young, but old enough. He also had to do some calculating to figure out how close her blood was to his. He knew a couple of families where first cousins got married and they inevitably lost many children in childbirth and some who grew up strange. However, Margarita was not his first cousin for Uncle Giuseppe was not really Josep's uncle, for it was common in this village to call an older relative Uncle. Josep used some pebbles to draw a family tree and figured that Margarita's father was his second cousin. That seemed distant enough. A week went by and Josep spent time looking for his goats that wandered away from him, returning to doors that he had incredibly forgotten to shut, and finding himself wondering where he was and what he was waiting for. His mother had to remind him to eat. On Sunday, he got to church early, but did not go in. Instead, he waited for Uncle Giuseppe's family to arrive and stepped in line behind them hoping to join them at service. But the pews at San Rocco only held three, so Josep settled in behind Margarita and all those feelings he had the week before reemerged and again the mass went unobserved. This went on for three more weeks. Food had no taste. Nothing was of interest except his second cousin once removed whose image and smell he could not expel from his thoughts. Finally, his mother insisted he tell her what the problem was. She did not want to see her son return to Grappa. Not able to keep his feelings welled up inside himself one more second; he poured his feeling for Margarita out to his mother. "You fool, just go ask for her hand." "But, I am tongue tied in her presence." "No, no, you must ask Uncle Giuseppe. It would not be acceptable to ask Margarita. I think he will say yes. After all, she will not find a husband in this community who has as much to offer as you have." Josep asked, Giuseppe said "Of course" and Margarita was delighted to marry into the respectable Pedretti family to a man who was old enough he would not turn again to the bottle or to his friends to escape his responsibility to her. Two weeks later, on January 25 in the year of our lord 1688, Father Francesco Gadola officiated at the wedding of Josep [age 33], son of Guglielmo Pedretti and Margarita Lombardini, to Margarita [age 14], daughter of Giuseppe and Joanna Gadola, at the San Bernardo parish church. Every individual who lived in the four settlements of San Bernardo attended what we might call today "the wedding of the century." Josep spared no expense to make his young bride happy. He even hired a cook from the Red Rooster Tavern in Chiavenna, the first ever for San Bernardo, to provide the food. While there were a few jokes about the town drunk making good and winter marrying spring, no one remembered or would ever witness a party like this one. The closest they came to such a party was held twenty-five years later when Josep and Margarita again invited everyone from the five hamlets of San Bernardo, namely Salina, Scannabecco [aka San Rocco], La Palu, Martinon and Pescosta to celebrate their twenty-fifth anniversary. It was January 25, 1713. The towns-people woke to a glowing sun rising over the mountain to the southeast. The bishop from Como had arrived the evening before and had prayed at Vespers for a balmy day to celebrate the Silver Anniversary of this couple who had become respected elders of their community and vocal supporters of the reign of the Bishop of Como. The Council of Val San Giacomo had approved the villages request to make this day a local holiday. The day began with a high mass with Fr. Signorelli being joined by the pastor of Olmo to assist in the ceremony conducted by Bishop Giuseppe Olgiati. During his sermon, Bishop Olgiati praised the couple as the shining brow of his archdiocese. He called upon Jesus to bless this couple that had so blessed the earth by their life of compassion. He declared from the pulpit, "Theirs is a story that needs to be told. In this hall there must be a poet and I call upon you to sing of their life, I call upon you to find the words to immortalize their love story, I call upon you to let their story be one to be emulated for centuries to come."

The young Bishop, who had been appointed Bishop of Como one year and 364 days earlier, then prayed to Jesus to allow all who were gathered to return in 25 years to celebrate the Golden Anniversary of Josep Pedretti and Margherita Gadola. There were some in church who were repelled by what they considered a blasphemous call for a favor from Jesus and that the couple would now be cursed. Two days later, Margherita was dead as were three other guests of the wedding. While most wanted to blame the curse put on them by the Bishop, the four died of food poisoning brought on by some improperly cured bresaola. When Josep died in his 70th year on July 2, 1724, some 14 years shy of the golden anniversary that was not meant to be, many parishioners again recalled the jinx cast by the Bishop of Como. When word arrived in late 1736, less than two years shy of the cursed date, that the Bishop had mysteriously died, those who remembered the stir he made that day over 23 years before had no doubt that his maker had called him early for his audacity.

Herein is the record of Josep Pedretti's line. Josep lived for three score and ten years and he and Margarita begat six children whom they named Guglielmo, Maria Margarita, Jacobus, Bernardus, Josep Maria and Joanna who passed away from an unknown disease at the age of 15 months. Josep Maria, born in his father's forty-ninth year, took work at his uncle's grocery in Gordona at the age of 14. He worked there for 24 years, seemingly content and showing little interest in women or grappa. Then one day, a young lady from another town came into the store to purchase some of the famous Gordona bresaola. She was visiting her Uncle who lived in Gordona, and Josep Maria fell in love at first sight. Marta Maranese, the young lady from Chiavenna, was equally taken by the distinguished looking bachelor of Gordona, but she made it clear to him from the beginning that she would not live in Gordona under any circumstances. Josep Maria, already known as the man with the luck, took the coach into Chiavenna that weekend and found a job at Guanella's grocery. Three months later Josep Maria, son of Josep Pedretti and Margarita Gadola wed Marta, the daughter of Agostino and Lucrezia Maranese in S. Lorenzo Church in Chiavenna.

When Guglielmo (Josep Maria's oldest brother) was in his twenty-second year, he wooed Stephani Cerletti's daughter, Anna Maria, and one year later vowed to be ever faithful to her. This is the record of Anna Maria and Guglielmo's progeny. Anna Maria gave birth to her first child during a late blizzard on April 23, 1719 and they named her Margarita in the tradition of naming the eldest daughter after her father's mother. Two years later, they presented Margarita with a baby sister and they christened their newest baby Anna Maria Pedretti. Two years later they gave birth to the twins, Giuseppe and Maria. Some time passed before Anna Maria again found herself pregnant. She gave birth to Stefano on a cool overcast day on June 2, 1727 and was soon pregnant with Orsola born 18 months later. Their third son and seventh child had his first breath on the twelfth day of January 1730 and they christened him the next day with the name of his father, Guglielmo. Two years later, on June 17, 1732 Anna Maria, at age 42 gave birth to her last child who would not live to see his 42nd birthday. As was the custom Giuseppe inherited his father's home and tillable land. Stefano married a woman from Milan and settled there where he became known for his breeding animals. Giacomo, failing to woo a wife from the mountain town, joined a traveling performance troupe and was not heard from again until he returned to the San Bernardo in late 1772 where he died 3 days before Christmas in that year.

There is little known of Guglielmo II except that he also married a woman named Anna Maria Cerletti, who was of the other Cerletti family lineage. As his wife was an only child, Guglielmo inherited her father's livestock, land and home which was located on plat 392 in Salina. Guglielmo's descendants would live in this house for the next 100 years. The walls of the house, which burned in 1999, are still standing. Anna begat three daughters before baptizing, on February 16, 1753, their oldest son whom they named Guglielmo after the baby's grandfather. Even though Guglielmo only lived to be 56, he witnessed the burial of five of his six children [Only Guglielmo III outlived him] with two of his daughters tragically dying within three days of each other during the harsh winter of 1759.

This is the record of the line of Guglielmo III who married Maria Catarina Gadola the daughter of Francesco Gadola and Maria Pedretti, the daughter of Giovanni Antonio, on a bright sunshiny day on the sixth day of April in 1774. Over in Strasburg, Mozart was premièring his Symphony in A # 29 to celebrate the special occasion happening 3000 feet up on San Bernardo Mountain [Okay, I have to admit Mozart did not know he was playing for this lovely couple 300 miles away, but I am having fun thinking he played special for them all the same]. Maria Catarina and Guglielmo's eldest was born exactly one year later and was christened on the seventh day of April in 1775 as Guglielmo Maria Pedretti. He was known throughout his life as "Quarto." Twenty months later, Catarina gave birth to Anna Maria who married Giorgio Fanetti from Fraciscio, moved to that village, and worshipped at San Rocco of Fraciscio. Their next child whom they called Maria passed away three months and 24 days after she was baptized. As Quarto was sickly and not expected to live, his parents also named their fourth born Guglielmo Maria, who later gave birth to Giacomo who married Maria of San Bernardo, moved to Chiavenna and there six years after their wedding begot Carlo Giuseppe Maria Pedretti, born November 3, 1836, who grew up to lead the Society of Democratic Workers and fight for the rights of workers throughout the world. The people of Chiavenna honored their prominent son by naming a street Via Carlo Pedretti. The hundredth anniversary of Carlo Pedretti's death was celebrated on Thursday, the Seventh Day of May in the year of two thousand and nine. Four years after the birth of Guglielmo Maria the younger, Maria Catarina gave birth to her fifth child Francesco Antonio Maria and 2 and ½ years later her last child Maria was baptized in the San Bernardo Church.

The world was afire with agitation when Guglielmo "Quarto" was born. The people in the British colonies across the Atlantic were about to turn into insurgents in favor of independence. Although it took a few years before information about the revolution reached the mountain village of San Bernardo, by the time the British surrendered in 1781 and Guglielmo was old enough to understand what was happening, the news got to every village in Europe, including San Bernardo, within the month. Restlessness and rebellion were in the air. France, almost next door, broke into chaos as terrorists beheaded the King and Queen [16 Oct 1793] when Guglielmo Quarto was only 18. Talk of revolution filled the daily gossip at the water well. Guglielmo joined the Adelphi society and led the Mountain Brigade in the successful revolt from the century-long control of the area by the Swiss who were distracted by the growing revolutionary mood at home and the reputation of a young French general known by his first name who seemed invincible. Any hope of establishing a Chiavenna or Valtellina republic [Guglielmo favored the later] was undermined when Napoleon invaded Italy just months after the successful revolt and permanently squashed all hope of independence. On October 10, 1797 he ordered the entire area annexed to the Cisalpine Republic with headquarters in long-standing enemy Milan. Guglielmo and his Mountain Brigade had not fought for independence to see their dream annexed by an even more centralized government. For three months, Guglielmo led sporadic attacks on the devil invaders, but it soon became clear there was nothing to be done. Napoleon's army was invincible and even more damaging to Guglielmo's cause was the fact that the French developed a substantial following among local defectors who saw the advantages of unifying the area under the Cisalpine Republic. Napoleon assured the citizens of certain liberties long absent from their life, and the presence of the soldiers saw a virtual end of crime and thievery in the valley. With no support even from old Adelphi colleagues, the Brigade disbursed and the rebels returned to goat tending in the mountains. When word arrived that Napoleon's troops had begun to recruit single males under the age of 33 throughout the Valley, Guglielmo smirked, "I told you so" and, abhorred by the thought of fighting for the hated enemy, proposed marriage to Maria Anna, the daughter of Silvestro Paiarola and Maria Orsola, the daughter of the late Joanni Gadola. They exchanged vows at a small ceremony in San Rocco church on the following Saturday, May 25, 1803. To be safe, Guglielmo donated 16 masses to the San Bernardo's parish in order to get the pastor to falsify his birth documents to show he had been born in 1771. Soon it became obvious that living high in a poor isolated community had its advantages. The soldiers, who had conscripted hundreds of boys from Val San Giacomo, never bothered to climb the mountains for recruits. Nor did the citizens of San Bernardo ever hear from or see any representatives from the new Milanese government. Life on the mountain continued as before.

Maria Anna Paiarola was happy to marry Guglielmo for he came from an esteemed family, but she knew that he had not married her out of love. She slept in Guglielmo's house that night, but she did not sleep in his bed. Night after night he indicated to her that she should sleep in the bed in the room for the children while he crawled alone into his bed. After a month, Maria Anna's mother, Maria Orsola came by to find out how her daughter was doing and Maria Anna broke into tears. Orsola, the name by which Maria Orsola was known, told Anna to be patient, Guglielmo would learn to love her but she would have to woo him. But what to do? She had never wooed a man. Until Guglielmo kissed her at the altar after saying, "I do" she had never been kissed by a man. "Mom, it is still the only kiss I have received." Orsola placed her arms around Maria Anna and held her close. Seeing that her daughter was inconsolable, Orsola did what no San Bernardo mother ever did before or since. She offered to tell Maria Anna how she had successfully wooed her father. But only on one condition; she could never reveal her secrets to anyone, not even her own children. Good for her promise, Maria Anna never repeated those stories and they went to the grave with her.

Maria Anna proved a worthy student and Guglielmo was seduced within the month. Nine months after the first night they slept together a burly baby boy emerged from Maria Anna's womb and was baptized with the name Guglielmo Maria the next day on April 17, 1804 by Father Christopherus Lombardini. Soon Maria Anna was happily pregnant again. The love between Quarto and Maria Anna grew deeper and deeper by the day. Quarto began to enjoy doing the small things for Maria Anna that made her pregnancy more comfortable. In the eighth month, he began to tie her shoelaces in the morning before heading to the stable. In the evening, he laid his head on her belly to feel his newest child's kicks. He woke with Anna in the dark of night and walked her to the outhouse after the baby kicked her bladder. Their second child, Maria Caterina, was born on the twenty first day of November in 1806. On July 4, 1826, she married her brother's wife's brother, Stephanus Maria Camillus Cerletti and they begat Giacomo who begat Giochino who begat Amedeo who begat Alberto Cerletti, who performed much of the research into both the Cerletti and Pedretti ancestry.

Quarto and Maria Anna also begat Silvestre Joannes Bonus, Francisco Maria, Maria Orsola (who was named after her grandmother). Their sixth child, Antonius Maria born in 1815 died in 1820 of yellow fever as did his younger sister Marianna [born May 6, 1818] and younger brother Giovanni Maria [Born December 17, 1819] who died exactly three months after being baptized in the San Rocco Chapel. Ironically that year on May 12, shortly after the death of Giovanni Maria, 175 miles south of San Bernardo Florence Nightingale was born. Her later discoveries, if known at the time, might have saved the lives of these three children. Guglielmo lived to see his son take over the Pedretti farm which had been in the family name since they had arrived in San Bernardo over four hundred years earlier. Shortly thereafter he died content in his sleep. His wife, heartbroken and disoriented, died a month later after falling down the hay hole in their stable.

Life on the San Bernardo Mountain was never better than during the youth of young Guglielmo V "Quinto". The unification of the entire region under Milano rule bought peace and posterity to the valley below. While people worried when Napoleon renamed the area the Kingdom of Italy and proclaimed himself King when the Guglielmo V was only one, there was no noticeable change on the mountain or in the San Giacomo Valley. The continued increase of trade over the Spugen pass brought prosperity to the entire valley and provided new opportunities for the men of San Bernardo to both sell their wares for good money, and to get winter jobs and greatly supplement their families' income. Even after the malevolent Austrians occupied the entire region after Waterloo, that area prospered and peace reigned. The Typhus fever, that killed so many that same year, stayed off the mountain. High in the mountains, the population suffered none of the loss of freedom and independence that those living in the valley felt. Guglielmo V was free to roam the mountains and traverse from village to village. His closest playmate was Teresa, the daughter of his aunt Margherita who had married Stefano

Cerletti and lived in the beautiful Cerletti quarters located on the right bank of Selene, the middle zone of San Bernardo. The two met early in the morning and disappeared into the hills for hours. They never seemed to lack for things to do together. When Father Lombardini started a school in Pescosta, the lowest zone of San Bernardo, Guglielmo stopped at Teresa's house and they skipped down the hill laughing all the way to the San Bernardo church hall. When the weather was good they studied in Teresa's yard and when the weather was not so good, they sat on the floor before her fireplace pouring over the latest lessons Father had given them.

At seventeen, Guglielmo V got restless and joined a band of young Italians who first initiated the idea of a Unified Italy. While his father had been fervently opposed to this approach, Quarto had come to see the advantages of unification and had completely reversed his youthful desire to see the San Giacomo Valley be an independent country. He was proud to see his son join the cause but equally apprehensive to see his son getting in arms way of danger.

After three years of futile struggle, Guglielmo V returned to his parent's mountain. Guglielmo' first stop was to see his best friend Teresa. She opened the door and he saw neither his friend nor his cousin, but a woman with a smile that made his knees collapse under him. Teresa was equally taken by this young man fresh back from the struggle for unification who looked completely in charge. Their hikes through the woods turned into romantic outings that led to the exchanging of vows before their families at San Bernardo church on June 10, 1824. Teresa's aunt, Marianna Cerletti who had married Giovanni Battista Buzzetti on August 18, 1791 attended the wedding with her daughter and son-in-law Francesco and Teresa Zaboglio along with their six-month-old baby, Marianna. Twenty-three years later, Marianna married Bartolomeo Sterlocchi and begat Madeline Sterlocchi on April 18, 1849. The Sterlocchis immigrated to Genoa, Wisconsin where Madeline fell in love with and married John Venner shortly after her sixteenth birthday.

Ten months after their wedding on April 8, 1825, Teresa Cerletti-Pedretti gave birth to their first son, properly named Guglielmo. This Guglielmo, who was sometimes called "Sesto," would be the first in 12 generations of Pedretti first born that did not settle into the Gadola House in San Rocco. He and his two brothers, Stefano, born on August 15, 1826 and Silvestro, born next in line on December 5, 1828 went adventuring the year after their mother died. As soon as the snow melted on their mountain in the spring of 1854, they left for the United States.

Fifteen months after Silvestro was baptized, Lorenzo, who would stay home and inherit his father's property, was born. Then Teresa gave birth to a sickly child who was given the name of Marianna to honor Guglielmo's mother, but she was not destined to see her first birthday. Two years later on August 20, 1830, a healthy baby girl was born to Guglielmo and Teresa and they also named her Marianna, in memory of her deceased sister. Bernardo come forth to announce the new year in 1834 and was followed two years later by Antonio. Then a stillborn child was followed 15 months later by Margherita, who later married Joseph Donacelli of Sommarovina. Maria Teresa, named for her mother, arrived on schedule on February 17, 1840 and Maria Orsola, who would marry Baptiste di Stefano, arrived on the cold bitter night of October 13, the following year. Maria Caterina, Maria, and Francesco (who would immigrate to South America), came along like clockwork.

With such a large family, Teresa spent much of her time in her garden. Because land was scarce, Teresa's garden was necessarily small, but her yield was large. In the fall and winter, Teresa gathered leaves, leftovers from the table, clippings, dead grass and stored it in the corner of the stable. Each week, she mixed the pile with some forkfuls of manure. When Guglielmo V replaced the bedding for the animals, he tossed the old straw onto the pile. At the first thaw, Guglielmo V and Teresa hauled this mixture along with some fresh manure to Teresa's garden, which was 450 meters from their stable. They loosened the top 3 inches of soil, and mixed it with one part fresh manure and three parts compost. Teresa let this mixture combine for at least ten days and then the first day the weather permitted she planted cabbage, peas, lettuce, rocket, curled parsley, sorrel and a wide variety of herbs. Once all threat of frost was over, Teresa completed her herb garden and planted potatoes, tomatoes, sweet corn, and ground cherries. She measured the location of every single seed she planted so that she did not waste even one centimeter of ground where she could raise a crop. Each year she moved the seeds a little closer until the yield suffered from over planting, and then she widened the seeding to the exact centimeter that permitted her to have the largest yield. She went to her garden every day to hoe so the weeds did not suck the nutrition away from her plants. As Teresa refined her growing techniques, her yields grew just as her family was growing. Still, Teresa could not get enough food so Guglielmo gave her forty square meters of the corner of his field used to grow feed for the cattle in the winter. In order to have enough food for the cattle, Guglielmo cleared a third of an acre of forest on the far reaches of the land. The mountain was so steep and rocky that no one but Guglielmo thought it possible to grow anything there. One rock at a time, Guglielmo moved the rocks from the upper half of the plot to the lower half until the land was level enough to tile. Then he went further into the woods past his new "farm" and scraped enough soil loose to cover his plot with dirt to grow winter wheat.

Teresa was especially gifted at raising ground cherries and she put them in her salads, made jam, and used them to garnish many dishes. Still she had ground cherries left. One year when the apple trees were barren, Teresa decided she would use some of the ground cherries that had been so plentiful that year in place of apples for the ingredients of her pie. Her first pies were bitter, but her children ate them. Guglielmo said, "It's not your apple pie, but not bad for a substitute." The next time she made a pie using ground cherries, Teresa added a little more sugar. And the next time a little more sugar, until she got it just right. Soon, her children were asking only for her ground cherry pies and inviting their friends over to taste the new pie their mother had created. She had to make twice as many pies until she gave her recipe to every woman in the village. The next year, every gardener on the mountain of San Bernardo planted extra ground cherry plants for the pies that would fill the air with their mouth-watering aroma in the fall. To this day, many of Teresa's progeny unwittingly reproduce her recipe to the delight of all who taste this distinctive delicacy.

Teresa experimented in her garden in order to feed her growing family. She also spent time there because she loved being in the open, feeling the dirt between her fingers, pulling the "evil" weeds so that her "good" children could flourish. She basked in the sunshine and gloried in the harvest, picking each ground cherry, pea, bean, and potato hill with the care a jeweler gave to shaping a diamond. She dug each potato hill with her bare hands to assure that not one tuber would be damaged. She often thought, "My garden is as close to heaven as I will ever get."

Teresa was closer to heaven than she dreamed, for her God came calling for her on January 29, 1853, just five short years after her baby Francesco had been born. With their mother gone, too many siblings to feed, and the fear of being conscripted by the Austrian army to fight a war they did not believe in, accompanied by the lure of the new Campodolcino settlement in the United States, Teresa's three eldest sons, Guglielmo VI, Stefano and Silvestro, struck out for America. First, they went to Paris via Airolo, Switzerland where Stefano made a last good bye and a promise to the love of his life, Adelaide Lombardi, that he would bring her to America before the end of the next year. They walked and hitchhiked their way to Paris and on to La Havre where they boarded the *Connecticut* that was mostly full of Germans but also a few Frenchmen, all headed to New York to find the land of gold. The Pedretti boys knew there was no gold, but they knew there was land to be had (all but free from the government) to begin farms in a far western place called Bad Ax City in Bad Ax County in a territory they thought was called Wastecon Sin. It did not have an appealing name, but they had friends from Campodolcino who had settled there the previous year and had sent back news there was an abundant amount of land to be had for ambitious young men. And these three, if they were anything, were restless and ambitious.

In the year before Walt Whitman published *Leaves of Grass* [1855] they docked in New York City on August 23, got jobs driving oxen-pulled-wagons west until they arrived in Chicago where they stayed for a week before making their way to Bad Ax City, Wisconsin. Arriving late in the year 1854, they constructed a barn-house just below the recently completed Morelli house which was one of the first houses built in Bad Ax City. After a long hard winter, Guglielmo, now going by the name Wilhelm, told his brothers he was going west to California where he could raise vegetables and fruits. Some years later, he posted a letter to his brothers in Bad Ax City telling them that he had arrived safely, changed his name to the more American William and had started a dairy farm with 30 cows. By 1869 he had relocated to Chile where he married, Maria Petrona Rios on 15 November 1869. Earlier he had sired with Maria Rios a bastard boy and they named him Ramon, thus ending the long string of Guglielmos. Later his younger brother emigrated to Chile to be with his eldest brother.

One year after arriving Stephen sent for Adelaide and they were married in Romance, an outlying community of the idyllic town of Harmony, Wisconsin, on February 26, 1856. This is a record of Stephen and Adelaide's line. They begat William who begat Jessie, Peter who farmed the original farm; Mary who became a nun; Stephen who married Marie Ursula, the daughter of John Battista Levi of Fraciscio and Elizabeth Fanetti and with her begot Steven, Elizabeth, John, Phillip, Joseph who became the mayor of Genoa, Joffre, Madeline and Beatrice. Stephen and Adelaide's last child, Madeline, childless her entire live, was born eight months before Stefano's premature death under a timber meant for his new barn. Stephen and Adelaide's twenty grandchildren begot them 121 great grandchildren [One of them brings you this story] who in turn begot 331 offspring; too many for us to consider here. Each of them shares with me the genes of Stefano Pedretti and Adelaide Lombardi. They are my cousins but they are no more to me than you are. Like them, you are my family. This is our story, as much your story as mine.

Stefano and Adelaide's second son Peter married Margaret Malin born in Pennsylvania and they begat Stephen who never married, Joseph who drowned in the Mississippi river, William who married Agnes Venner and was a farmer as were his brothers Peter, Alois, Albert, Victor (who married a Berra whose family had come from outside of Milan), and Paul. After Paul, Peter and Margaret begat Mary who married Francis son of Bartholomew Venner, Margaret who married a Levi whose family was from Fraciscio and Ada who married a man whose family was not from Italy. His children gave him 74 grandchildren and they gave him 258 great grandchildren.

December 15, 1951

Peter (son of Stefan and Adelaide) lived four score and ten years and three hundred and twenty-four days. Peter lived to see children of the fourth generation. The children of Little Agnes, Anna Mae, Clara, Alvin and Carol sat at his bedside learning the story of our stories. Peter died on Saturday, December 15, 1951 the week that Dwight Eisenhower declared he was a Republican; the New Yorker cover featured a typical small town in America getting ready for Christmas, Charlie Brown frightened Lucy as he headed out back to repair the roof (that is the roof on his doghouse), the radio show Dragnet premièred on national Television and Desi Arnaz shocked America by speaking a few Cuban words in the much beloved TV show "I Love Lucy." Peter died while staying in his son's home. The funeral procession carrying his body for final services at St. Charles and burial in the church cemetery in Genoa, Wisconsin is reported to have been two miles long.

-To be continued for a few more centuries –

Post Script: Peter's wife Maggie gave birth to eleven children who begat 73 children who made 263 great-grandchildren for Peter and Maggie - the last who was born on the 23rd day of March in the year 1995 of the Current Era.

William Charles Pedretti , the third born son of Peter married Agnes, the eldest daughter of Bartholomew and Mary Caroline Venner on November 22, 1922 and they begat Little Agnes who passed to her Maker in the year of our Lord two thousand and eight, Ann who emigrated with her husband Paul to western Canada, Claire who died from Cancer, Bernard who rented his first farm at age 14, Dolores who lives in the town where Lewis and Clark first saw the Pacific Ocean, Joseph baked a million Danish rolls, Margaret who never married, Joan who begat two girls, William George who owns to this day the farms that his great grandfathers staked out over 150 years ago, Mary Jane who begat a composer, designer, teacher and outdoor lover, Daniel who never wanted, Michael who composed the information you are reading, James and John who died in their first week on earth, and Leo who was never sucked into the work ethic black hole that has robbed meaning from the American people and whose understanding of the meaning of life urgently needs to be recorded for posterity and adhered to by the next generation if America is to recapture its integrity. William and Agnes' children begat 71 children - the creative work of several will be included in Book XII of The Story of Our Stories.

Postcard of Genoa probably taken in 1860s. The building in the middle is believed to have served as the first home and stable of the Pedretti brothers

Clara,Carol,Carl,Alvin,Agnes,Ray,Bernard,Lawrence

Mary Lee Stowe held by Marie,Ann,Pat held by Frank,Lucy,
Marvin,Dolores,Don,Shirley Levi,Terese,Arni

Ron,Ralph,Geraldine Levi,Joan,Marge,Jim P.,Jim V., Joe,
Bill,Rita,Marilyn

to the right of Grandpa Pete): Bob,Donna Levi,Duane,Ken,
Berneal

Tom V.,Ed,Dan,Mary Jane,Dorothy

Peter Pedretti Eightieth Birthday celebration
Photo taken with 43 grandchildren
Summer 1941
Back Row Clara, Carol, Carl, Alvin, Agnes,
Ray, Bernard, and Lawrence
Third Row: Mary Lee Stowe held by Marie, Ann,
Pat held by Frank, Lucy, Marvin, Dolores, Don,
Shirley Levi, Teresa, and Arni
Second Row: Ron, Ralph, Geraldine Levi, Joan, Margaret, Jim, Jim
Venner, Joe, Bill, Rita, Marilyn, Grandpa Peter, Bob, Donna Levi,
Duane Venner, Ken, and Berneal
Sitting: Tom Venner, Ed, Dan, Mary Jane, and Dorothy
Note: If only first name given, the last name is Pedretti

Another picture of Peter Pedretti and 43 of his grandchildren gathered to celebrate Peter's 80th birthday – Peter's children would give birth to 30 more offspring – giving Peter 73 grandchildren.

William and Agnes Pedretti Family 1937
Back Row: Agnes, Ann, Clara, Bernard
Front Row: Dolores, Joseph, Margaret, Joan
Sitting: William
Agnes would give birth to six more children

BOOK III

THE BEGETTERS OF CHILDREN

Addenda

Ahnentafel Chart for Stefano Maria Pedretti

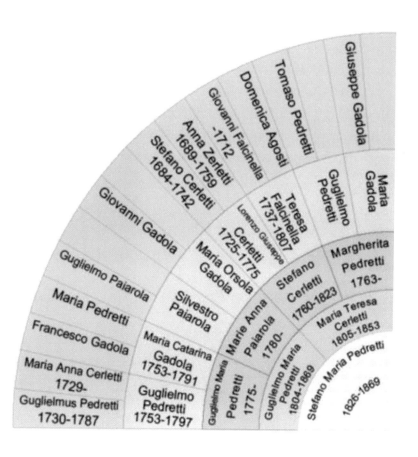

Meet Stefano Maria Pedretti's ancestors, all of whom were born, lived and died in San Bernardo; a small mountain village located about 100 miles north of Milano. Our story traces his paternal linage back 8 generations to his great-great-great-great-great grandfather Guglielmo Pedretti of whom we know little except his wife gave birth to Giuseppe Pedretti in 1654. The Pedretti name was first recorded as being used by Guglielmo, the son of Petro Godola, in the year of 1553. It is highly likely that the first man to use the surname Pedretti was our Guglielmo's grandfather and that Guglielmo was named after him as was the tradition at the time.

The Godola family first immigrated to San Bernardo around 1100 joining and soon intermarrying with the original settlers who arrived here around 800, therefore Stefano could trace his roots back to the original settlers.

Ancestors & Descendants of Stefano Maria Pedretti

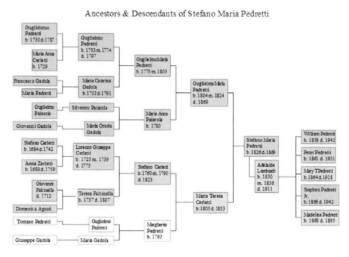

This is the list of all known ancestors as of publication of Stefano Maria Pedretti, born 15 August, 1826. The ancestors are presented in the strict numbering order created and first used by Michaël Eytzinger in 1590. This table includes the full name of each ancestor as well as the dates and places of birth, marriage, and death if known.

The First Generation

1. Stefano Maria PEDRETTI was born on 15 August 1826 in San Bernardo, Sondrio, Italy. He died on 1 April 1869 in Genoa, Wisconsin. He is buried in St Charles Cemetery, Genoa, Wisconsin

Stefano, the second child of Guglielmo Maria Pedretti and Maria Teresa Cerletti, was so fast and agile - skipping nimbly across the mountainside - he was given the nickname "Camoscin". In San Bernardo, when a person was agile and fast in mountain trails, he was compared to a chamois ("You are fast as a chamois"). Camoscin with his brothers William "Guglielmo" and Sylvester came to the US on the ship Connecticut which departed from Le Havre, France and arrived in New York on 23 August 1854. They arrived in Bad Ax [later named Genoa] Wisconsin in the fall of 1854 and immediately built a home, more barn than house, on the south side of the road that would later lead to the Catholic Church. It is believed that the brothers worked in the lumber business, chopping trees, making firewood for the steam ships that refueled in Bad Ax and cutting trees into planks at the lumber mill. On February 8, 1858, Stefano married Adelaide Lombardi, a recent immigrant from Airolo, Switzerland. Their marriage license was issued in Harmony Township, Bad Ax County (now Vernon County) on February 6, 1858. Most likely Stefano and his bride shared the original "Pedretti" house with Sylvester and William [who moved to California before 1860], as there is no reason to believe they could have afforded their own home prior to the time they purchased 40 acres in section 27 and built a log cabin there around 1868. According to the one-paragraph biography written for the 80th birthday of Stefano's son, Peter, the family moved to a farm along highway 56 at this time. Stefano built a log cabin near the creek at the foot of the hill near the Northwest corner of the West ½ of the SE ¼ of section 27 in township 13 [Genoa township].

Shortly thereafter, Stefano was killed by a lumber-related accident on April 1, 1869. According to Jim Venner's *The Descendants of Francesco Zaboglio*, Stefano "died from being crushed by a timber while building a barn." The story that passed down through the descendants of Peter's brother Stephen Pedretti is that Stefano was killed while cutting logs for the railroad. Another great grandchild, Ann Pedretti-Reindl wrote, "The story I heard about Stephen's death was that a log fell on him when he was building a house." Fred Pedretti's website states Stefano was "killed hauling cordwood in 1869." Peter's 80th birthday "biography" states "When he was 8 years old his father was killed by a timber." Stefano was only 42 years old. Since Adelaide lived on the farm for some time after his death, the neighbors must have completed the building. He was one of the first to be buried in the St. Charles cemetery in Genoa, Wisconsin. His tombstone reads, "STEPHEN PEDRETTI/ NATIVE OF ST BERNARD, ITALY/ DIED APRIL 1, 1869/ AGED 43 YEARS/ He left a wife and five children." His wife, 38 years old, was left to raise their five children, William [age 11], Peter [8], Mary T. [5], Stephen [3] and Madeline [8 months]. Stefano and Adelaide's story is told in Book VI.

Stefano married **Adelaide LOMBARDI** daughter of Peter LOMBARDI and Magdalene FORNI on 26 February 1856 in Harmony, Bad Axe, Wisconsin. Adelaide was born on 28 July 1830 in Airolo, Ticino, Switzerland. She died on 10 February 1911 in Genoa, Wisconsin. She was buried on 13 February 1911 in St Charles Cemetery, Genoa, Wisconsin. Book VI includes several letters Adelaide sent to Stefano.

Second Generation

2. **Guglielmo Maria PEDRETTI** was born on 17 April 1804 in San Bernardo, Sondrio, Italy. He died on 1 December 1869 in San Bernardo, Sondrio, Italy. He married Maria Teresa CERLETTI on 10 June 1824 in San Bernardo, Sondrio, Italy.

3. **Maria Teresa CERLETTI** was born on 27 January 1805 in San Bernardo, Sondrio, Italy. She gave birth to 15 children and was survived by all but two. She died on 29 January 1853 in San Bernardo, Sondrio, Italy. Her story is told in Book V.

Third Generation

4. **Guglielmo Maria PEDRETTI** was born on 7 April 1775 in San Bernardo, Sondrio, Italy. He died in San Bernardo,

Sondrio, Italy. He married Marie Anna PAIAROLA on 25 February 1803.

5. **Marie Anna PAIAROLA** was born on 21 April 1780 in San Bernardo, Sondrio, Italy.

6. **Stefano CERLETTI** was born on 17 September 1760 in San Bernardo, Sondrio, Italy. He died on 4 January 1823 in San Bernardo, Sondrio, Italy. He married Margherita PEDRETTI on 22 September 1790.

7. **Margherita PEDRETTI** was born on 25 November 1763 in San Bernardo, Sondrio, Italy.

Fourth Generation

8. **Guglielmo PEDRETTI** was born on 16 December 1753. He died on 4 October 1797. He married Maria Catarina GADOLA on 6 April 1774.

9. **Maria Catarina GADOLA** was born on 9 October 1753. She died on 13 February 1791.

10. **Silvestro PAIAROLA** married Maria Orsola GADOLA.

11. **Maria Orsola GADOLA.**

12. **Lorenzo Giuseppe CERLETTI** was born on 8 December 1725 in San Bernardo. He died on 17 January 1775. He married Teresa FALCINELLA on 17 September 1759 in San Bernardo, Sondrio, Italy.

13. **Teresa FALCINELLA** was born on 6 October 1737 in San Bernardo. She died on 16 August 1807.

14. **Guglielmo PEDRETTI** married Maria GADOLA.

15. **Maria GADOLA.**

Fifth Generation

16. **Guglielmus PEDRETTI** was born on 12 January 1730. He died on 19 June 1787. He married Maria Anna CERLETTI.

17. **Maria Anna CERLETTI** was born on 28 May 1729.

18. **Francesco GADOLA** was born in San Bernardo married Maria PEDRETTI.

19. **Maria PEDRETTI.**

20. **Guglielmo PAIAROLA.**

22. **Giovanni GADOLA.**

24. **Stefano CERLETTI** was born in 1684 in San Bernardo. He died on 23 April 1742. He married Anna ZERLETTI.

25. **Anna ZERLETTI** was born in 1689 in San Bernardo. She died on 24 March 1759.

26. **Giovanni FALCINELLA** died on 2 May 1712. He married Domenica AGOSTI.

27. **Domenica AGOSTI.**

28. **Tomaso PEDRETTI.**

30. **Giuseppe GADOLA.**

Sixth Generation

32. **Guglielmo PEDRETTI** was born on 22 March 1694. He died on 8 September 1758. He married Anna Maria CERLETTI.

33. **Anna Maria CERLETTI** was born in 1690. She died on 5 May 1756.

34. **Stefano CERLETTI** was born in 1684 in San Bernardo. He died on 23 April 1742. He married Anna ZERLETTI.

35. **Anna ZERLETTI** was born in 1689 in San Bernardo. She died on 24 March 1759.

36. **Antonio GADOLA.**

38. **Giovanni Antonio PEDRETTI.**

48. **Stefano CERLETTI** married Anna Maria GADOLA.

49. **Anna Maria GADOLA** was born in 1651. She died on 27 January 1727.

50. **Giorgio ZERLETTI** was born in 1649 in San Bernardo. He died on 4 August 1705. He married Anna PEDRONI.

51. **Anna PEDRONI** was born in 1666 in Gallivaggio. She died on 21 March 1726.

52. **Giovanni FALCINELLA.**

54. **Cristoforo AGOSTI.**

56. **Giogio PEDRETTI** died on 18 July 1840.

Seventh Generation

64. **Giuseppe PEDRETTI** was born in 1654. He died on 2 July 1724. He married Margherita GADOLA on 25 January 1688.

65. **Margherita GADOLA** was born in 1673. She died on 27 January 1713.

66. **Stefano CERLETTI.**

68. **Stefano CERLETTI** married Anna Maria GADOLA.

69. **Anna Maria GADOLA** was born in 1651. She died on 27 January 1727.

70. **Giorgio ZERLETTI** was born in 1649 in San Bernardo. He died on 4 August 1705. He married Anna PEDRONI.

71. **Anna PEDRONI** was born in 1666 in Gallivaggio. She died on 21 March 1726.

98. **Giovanni GADOLA.**

100. **Lorenzo ZERLETTI.**

102. **Guglielmo PEDRONI.**

Eighth Generation

128. Guglielmo PEDRETTI.
130. Giacoma GADOLA.
138. Giovanni GADOLA.
140. Lorenzo ZERLETTI.
142. Guglielmo PEDRONI.
200. Laurenti ZERLETTI.

Ninth Generation

280. Laurenti ZERLETTI.

The home of Guglielmo and Maria burned in 1999

San Bernardo

San Giacomo Filippo, Sondrio Lombardia, Italia

San Bernardo, a village located on Mt. Saint Bernard, is the original home of the Pedretti Family. The hamlet is an outlying post of the municipality of San Giacomo one of three political divisions that share the Saint James Valley which is located just north of Chiavenna.

San Bernardo, the village
A Frazione [subdivision] of the:
Municipality of San Giacomo Filippo
Province [county] of Sondrio
Region [state] of Lombardy
Country of Italy
Altitude: 1099-1242 meters [3614-4075 feet]
Coordinates: 46 ° 20 '47 "N, 9 ° 21' 23" E

This is the story of a mountain village located on Mt. San Bernardo

It is 1853. Eighty-three miles due north of Milan on a mountainside over 3600 feet above sea level, 300 people, 80 cows, 600 sheep and half that many goats wrestle their existence from steep, rocky fields that had been farmed and pastured for a thousand years. Land is so scarce the bones of the dead are dug up and stored in a crypt in order for the new dead to receive proper burial in the small graveyard just below the Church of San Bernardo, and the cows and sheep are driven higher into the mountains each summer so that the land near the village can produce enough fodder to feed the animals during the harsh winters. But the land, over-farmed for so many centuries, is unable to be bountiful.

In a small house on plat number 392 in Selene, one of the four districts that makes up the small village of San Bernardo that is part of the political community of Val San Giacomo, a family with 15 children mourns the loss of their mother who died on January 9th, just 18 days shy of her 48th birthday and only three weeks after her baby, Francesco, turned four. The family is deeply stressed by the loss of the woman that managed to keep them together through good years and bad. Even though the older boys travel to Chiavenna, Milan and beyond to work summers to bring home food and goods, the effort to keep the family together and in food and shelter has been shattered. In the spring, the three eldest boys meet secretly and discuss what they must do to ensure their family can survive the next winter.

The eldest, Guglielmo Pedretti, is the rightful heir of the house and stable on plat number 392 and the plots just outside of the village center that his family has owned and farmed for centuries. "Why would I want it?" he asks his two younger siblings. "There is nothing here I want. This place is literally hell frozen over. How and why did our ancestors ever move here and why did they stay?" he asked rhetorically. Stefano, not willing to let that denouncement go unchallenged, piped in, "there was reason enough to settle on "Monti di Vergogna [The original name for Mt. San Bernardo]. Our forerunners had had enough of avarice, wars, pestilence, thievery and floods. So they came here, where beauty replaced malice, freedom replaced serfdom, healthy air replaced plagues, caring replaced avarice where even Noah's waters could not reach, kindness replaced pilfering and satisfaction replaced wars."

Silvestre, the third child in the family, mutters, "Ah, the good old days."

Guglielmo, not wanting to miss the opportunity, says, "Si, si, si, this was a great place to live then. But now there are too many people and the land is worn to the bone. This land cannot support Dad and all of us. We have to leave. It is the only correct action. We must leave now and allow Dad and our younger brothers to eke a living off this barren land. Stefano, it is time to pack off to LeHavre and catch the first boat to the Americas." A year later they emigrate to Bad Ax, Wisconsin, USA.

San Bernardo, the village

1987

Photograph of San Bernardo taken in 1987 prior to the burning of former home of Guglielmo Pedretti's home. San Rocco is in background, Salina is in area marked by the rectangular box.

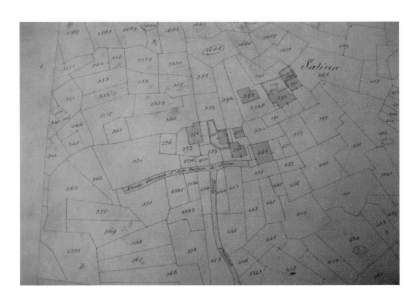

Plot of property in division of San Bernardo called Salina. Stefano Pedretti was born and raised in house located on plot 392.

Photo of what is left of the house on plat 392. This was the home of Guglielmo & Teresa Pedretti and their 13 living children. It burned in 1999.

Origins [800-1189]

Like many other villages in the Alps located 3,000 to 4,000 feet above sea level, San Bernardo was settled in the ninth or tenth century. The settlers chose to live in a remote, isolated mountainside where the land was rocky and steep, the forest had to be continually fought back, the growing season was too short for most vegetation, and the winters were long and harsh with residents snowbound for weeks on end. Travel from San Bernardo to the villages below for supplies and companionship was arduous and time consuming. The closest town, San Giacomo Filippo, is less than one mile as the crow flies but, to get up and down the mountain, the early residents had to extract a path that wove back and forth over five miles along the mountainside in order to make their way down to the valley to sell or trade their products for necessary supplies. Of course, getting down was the easy part. Loading supplies on one's back and trudging back up the mountain one step at a time was a grueling experience with some residents forgoing the goods and social interaction to avoid the encounter.

What did those first settlers escape from that made all of this worth it? They left behind the ravages of war, pestilence, and thieves on every corner and in every walk of life. Those thieves might have been bandits who took their possessions by force, soldiers who confiscated their goods and property [if they were lucky enough to own any], priests who demanded tithes and penalties for indulgences, and/or noblemen, the privileged class of the day, who were for the most part above the law and therefore could take what they wanted with impunity.

The Carolinian Empire, which had controlled the area since Charlemagne conquered it in 774, was declining.

Feudalism was creeping in with more and more commoner families conscripted into serfdom. As the empire declined, The Monastery of St. Dionysius challenged the Archbishop of Como for control of the area. The lengthy conflict led to Como maintaining religious power and the Monastery capturing the administrative and political power of both the Adda and Mera valleys which cover the vast area east of Lake Como. With this ongoing conflict, the populace was the ones to suffer. After their homes and farms were destroyed by the armies many had little choice but to submit to the role of serf; often to the very knights of armor who had impoverished them.

The locations for many mountain towns, including San Bernardo, were selected because they could not be seen from the valley below. The question comes to mind, were the settlers fugitives running from some horrific crime they had committed? The mountain area now known as Monti di San Bernardo was originally called Monti di Vergogna, the Mountains of Shame. A name like that probably did not come from the first residents, but was given to it by their neigbors and/or enemies. The name stuck, most likely because it represented some level of truth. This implies that the early settlers were fugitives and possibly ones on the shady side. One thing is sure, these early settlers (and their descendants for the next thousand years) found that this all but unreachable location offered protection from disease, natural disaster and human depravity.

The original settlers of San Bernardo chose a spot just above the reach of a mountain drainage area thereby providing, on one hand, water for their livestock and, on the other, protection from the spring floods. Nearly as important, there were one or more springs flowing out of the mountain providing constant and easy access to water for their drinking and cooking needs and for the animals when the gully ran dry. Water was essential for the survival of their livestock, themselves and for their everyday needs. San Bernardo and the area immediately surrounding the village also offered a sizable area of potentially tillable land, plenty of chestnuts and berries, and groves of larch trees that were valued for their building properties, meshed in with ash and birch trees that were needed for firewood, the fuel of necessity for cooking and heating. Even though there is a grand view of the valley below, before the fields were cleared and the church built, the sight was invisible from below, offering the residents the safeguard they needed. It seems likely that this mini-mesa already had a summer hut or two on it that would have been used for shelter by hunters who had for centuries combed these mountainsides for chamois and steinbecks. It is even possible that the first settlers had hunted these woods in the summers before they decided life in the valley or wherever they came from had become untenable.

Arriving on the mountain covered with ancient forests, the settlers had to immediately prepare for winter. They built year-round shelter and scrounged up food to carry them and their livestock through the winter. The original settlers arrived with few belongings, for certainly they were from the deprived class. Maybe they had a few rabbits and chickens and a pair of goats. There is no evidence that the settlers had access to beasts of burden, so whatever they had, they carried on their backs as they fled their former existence. Tools of any sort would have been sparse and prized so the settlers had to share whatever tools they had, an ax or two, a sickle, a spade, a couple of wedges and sledge maul; if they were lucky a mattock and maybe even a pickaxe. With these tools, heavy and dull compared to today's versions as it was not until a few centuries later that forging iron became sophisticated enough to make more efficient tools, the settlers had to till the land, cut down the tough larch trees, and split them to make joists and beams for their houses and stables. Branches were shaved to make fences to pen in the pigs and rabbits. They collected rocks and pulled them into place for foundations for homes and to build fireplaces for warmth and cooking indoors in the winter. Fields were cleared to provide for more grass and plantings to feed the domestic animals that were essential food as the hunt was not likely to provide enough meat to get through the winter. Even before doing these things, they had to cut down ash and birch trees to assure that the wood had time to dry to be used for firewood. There is every reason to believe those first years, especially the first winter, proved to be devastating and deadly to many settlers.

As was typical of the time, the citizens built their homes in a cluster around the village center and walked to their fields. No one built a house and barn on their own fields isolated from the rest of the community. Three primary reasons were: the individuals could better defend themselves against thieves and the enemy if they lived in close proximity, they would not be completely isolated when the snows covered the mountain side, and tillable land was too scarce to be using some of it for a house and stable.

Still, as the population increased, residents of San Bernardo spread the community out into four communes which were Streccia, Pos Costa, Martinon, and Scanabèch (now St. Rocco). While there would have been advantages for the population to huddle close in one locale to help survive the harsh winters, the advantages of separating into distinct wards outweighed the detriments. Among the reasons to develop separate hamlets, even though located within easy walking distance of each other, was to provide protection against the possibility of fire, an attack, or other disaster. If a fire should break out in one cluster of homes, the citizens had a better chance of containing it before it spread to the other areas than they would have if all the residents were grouped together. If attacked by the enemy or a gang of thieves, the residents of the other communes had at least some time to either form a resistance or escape. Also, areas of level ground flat enough to build a village were small; by building in four areas that permitted housing, they could each have enough room for a small garden, pens for their small animals and a stable for the livestock.

For the first two or three centuries, survival was an ongoing struggle. A growing population required them to constantly carve a few more square meters out of the forest. When a new home and stable was needed, the community worked together to build them. This was likely an ongoing endeavor as the town grew from a handful of houses to close to 50 homes by the end of the twelfth century. And the forest always resisted, doing its best to reclaim the cleared land with saplings taking root at every opportunity. The mountain frosts would spit rocks out of the ground that had to be cleared each spring. These were amassed along the lower edge of the fields to catch any runoff dirt and to help level out the fields over time. There was never enough land or vegetation to justify a horse or even a mule. So all farming was done by manual labor. The residents had to know about crops, raising animals, and using (and repairing) a wide variety of tools. "While there were some specialists for things like iron working, pottery and thatching, villagers had to possess among themselves the hundreds of different skills that made life possible, and perhaps a little enjoyable."[3]

Over time, those first settlers cut back the forest, discovered higher meadows to graze their sheep and goats in the summer months, built stone houses, increased their herds through breeding and carved a community out of that mountainside. To be sure, the mountainside was demanding, but it offered unsurpassed beauty and freedom from an enslaved environment where land could be confiscated and sons conscripted to support the soldiers of war and daughters raped by solders and the entitled.

Water

The importance of water cannot be overemphasized. One thousand feet above sea level, the settlers could not count on getting water from a local river. As stated above, they had to rely on the nearby gulley where water drained off the mountain, and a natural spring or two. Most likely one of their first actions was to build a dam to hold water to use for drinking, cooking, and laundry as they were aware that gullies and springs often dry up in late summer, so they would understand that they had to construct containers to store water. Since the water would seep away from any on-ground dam, they built troughs large enough to have water for themselves and their animals in times of drought. In order to get the water into the troughs they built the troughs around the spring. Later they

3 Nofi, Alfred, and James Dunnigan. "Commoners." *Medieval Life and the Hundred Years War.* 1997

blocked the area immediately surrounding the spring, leaving a hole in the middle of the block to force the water up, allowing them to catch the freshest water as it tumbled down from the apex.

Once they were settled into the village, they built a series of troughs letting the water fall from one trough to the next, not unlike the one shown in photo that still exists in San Rocco. The first trough provided water for drinking and cooking. The second trough was used to rinse clothes and other items they had cleaned in the bottom trough.

Livestock

The location was too high and too cold for orchards and much of the vegetation that was grown in the Po River Valley. The primary source of food for the mountaineers was from the eggs, milk and flesh of domesticated animals. This was supplemented with berries and chestnuts that grew wild. Lettuces, spinach and other greens that could have been grown in the cool climate with short summers was not part of the diet of Europeans at the time and it is unlikely it became part of the mountaineers' diet. The early settlers brought with them rabbits, chickens, goats and most likely pigs and sheep. Their primary occupation was breeding animals. Necessary to their survival was harvest off the tillable land near the village which was used to raise feed for the animals in the winter. Since tillable land was scarce, the women, with the help of the young boys in the village, herded the livestock up past the cultivated lands as soon as the weather broke in the spring. As the livestock depleted the available vegetation on each level and the snows melted and vegetation returned higher up the mountain, they pushed farther up the mountains, sometimes grazing as high as 6000 feet above sea level. The people of San Bernardo claimed collective grassing land on Mts. Alpe of Corneera, Lendine, Truzzo, Prosto, and Corzeca. In late August, they would slowly work their way back down the mountain eating everything in sight that had grown since they had ascended.

In the first centuries all the able-bodied women and children were needed to herd the sheep, goats and cows. Later they oversaw the pasturing of animals for farmers from the valley and other communities that had not laid claim to ownership of the mountainsides. The income from husbanding others' animals provided cash desperately needed to trade for goods with the merchants in the valley. Over the centuries, the citizens built summer huts along the grazing trails to provide shelter for the herders. Remnants of these shelters still exist. There were not a lot of pickings for the shepherds. Edible berries were scare that high in the mountains. Milk was plentiful and probably made the primary diet. To provide some variety, the shepherds learned to make cheese from the goat and lamb milk. From time to time, they butchered a lamb or calf. Much of the animal would be eaten in a timely fashion, but they did know how to smoke meat and all the basics necessary to smoke meat were available.

The men stayed below and tilled the land, gathered grasses, cut back more forests and built new shelters. The women too old to herd the animals maintained the gardens, cared for the chickens and pigs and cooked the meals.

The mountainside pastures and the larger groves of larch trees were owned in common by the citizens, for these had to be shared in order to pasture the livestock and provide lumber for building. But each family owned their own livestock, a stand of trees used mostly for firewood, less than 5 acres of tillable fields and a small plot in the village center on which sat their house, stable and a pen that was used to house pigs, chickens and rabbits. Most also had a shed to store firewood to keep it dry for fuel, and a small shack closer to the fields for tools etc. Stables were often built across the property from the home, sometimes attached to the neighbor's home. The typical stable was two stories, with the top story providing a hayloft to store food for the livestock for the winter, with the livestock sharing the lower level. In the winter, the farmers kept a path from their home to the stable where they milked the goats and cows twice daily, collected the eggs and made sure the animals were fed and watered. In the summer, the pigs, rabbits and chickens were penned near the house.

Once the fields thawed and the rains slowed enough for the fields to dry out and there was no threat of seeds and dirt being washed away, each farmer turned the soil and planted the year's crops. It is safe to say that about 75% of the land was used to raise tall grasses for hay. The smarter farmers probably tilled a different 25% of their land each year and planted rye and grass seed in the field. The first year the field yielded rye, which was cut down just before the first big frost. The next three years that section produced hay and then the cycle began all over again. By keeping this rotation, the farmers maximized the output while minimizing the cost for seed and the amount of labor. [It is true that medieval farmers elsewhere did not rotate crops. When a field became barren, it was allowed to lay fallow for one or more years before it was replanted. The farmers on San Bernardo could not afford to take some of their precious land out of service and so learned a simple but effective method of keeping their fields productive.] The farmers also spent considerable time keeping the forest back – digging out saplings that continued to want to recapture the mountain side. Twice a year the farmers would bring their scythe to their fields and cut the grasses. As the dew evaporated, they cut a swatch as big as they would be able to bundle and haul to their stable in one day. On the second day, they cut a second swatch, turned over the first to dry and at the end of the day raked into piles making it easier to bundle the next day. On the third day, they began again cutting the day's swath, and then they turned the patch cut the first day. Using a Spindle, a very cleverly designed [see picture] whittled tool, they threaded leather straps around a bundle of hay and then pulled the strap tight to form a bundle. After making a few bundles, they carried them to the stable, untied the bundles, stacked the hay and returned with the leather straps to repeat the process until the first day's crop was safely stored. As the sun set, they would rake up a patch of hay they would bundle up the next day. And so it went until all the grass was harvested. Grain was cut with a sickle. To the best of our knowledge, the same method was employed to bundle the grain harvest. The bundles were stacked to dry and when ready hauled to the village to be stomped on and shook until all the grain was separated from the fodder. An acre of rye produced at most three or four bushels of grain. [Today a mid-west farmer can get about 35 bushels/acre]. The villagers had stone wheels to grind the grain into flour. Since the grain stored better than flour, only enough was ground that was immediately used for bread or polenta [made from flour at that time] or could be safely stored. The kernels not immediately used for this purpose were stored in a cool place and used later to grind more flour and to feed the livestock.

Butchering was done in the fall after the weather turned cold. A typical family butchered a cow or steer, two pigs, and a goat and sheep or two. This provided for the best time to age, cure and store the meat for the winter months. While most of Europe relied on salted meat, salt was not easy to come by for these mountaineers so they learned early on to smoke their meat and air dry sausage and beef. Equally important, each farmer was interested in trimming the size of his herds so there were fewer mouths to feed over the winter. If they still had excess livestock, they drove them to the valley or neighboring villages and sold them to farmers or butchers. The farmers with the largest plots maintained the necessary studs to assure all were bred in season.

Chickens and rabbits were the primary source of meat in the summer. They were eaten the same day they were butchered, so no preservation means had to be devised. During the winter eggs were collected for food. As the weather improved, nests were prepared for the hens to lay eggs and the new pullets were carefully guarded from any downturns in the weather to assure their survival. Families could easily eat four or five chickens a week. With the hens averaging about six chicks per nest, some families kept as many as 20 chickens through the winter months.

Fuel

Trees necessary for cooking and heating their homes in the winter were plentiful. Each family owned a small grove located close to the village. Here a farmer chopped down the birch and ash trees, cut them up into manageable pieces, drug them to his yard and when weather did not permit him to work his fields or build their homes, he chopped the trees into pieces and split those into firewood. The wood was piled in lean-tos to further dry then moved before the snow fell to sheds built to keep it dry and accessible for winter fuel. Trees cut to clear forest became firewood for the church. When no clearing was necessary, each family contributed their fair share of firewood for the church and parsonage.

House Keeping

The families on the Mountains of Shame were self-sufficient and that self-sufficiency relied heavily on the ingenuity of the women of the village. They cooked the meals and tended to the care of the house. They spun the wool and wove the results into clothing and blankets. They tilled, planted and harvested the family garden. It was the women who tended and cared for the rabbits and chickens that provided so much of the family diet. In the spring, they joined their men in the fields clearing rocks and saplings. Not only did they free the men up for gathering firewood and food for the animals' winter needs by grazing the cattle on the mountain side, they participated actively in the butchering, cheese making, and gathering of nuts and berries that was so much a part of the fall preparation for winter. They harvested and brewed the herb-medicine remedies whose recipes were passed down from mother to daughter. Each house had a root cellar carved into the mountain side. Here the goods were carefully packed to provide "refrigeration" needed to make it through the winter. It has been said that life in northern Europe in this era was one of preparing for winter followed by persisting through the winter; and that was certainly true on the Mountains of Shame. It was the women of the community who took the lead in making sure the families were prepared, while the men tended to make sure the animals survived the winters. The mothers not only bore the children but were responsible for their care and education, nursing them through sickness, burying them when they could not, and making sure each child that grew up had a strong religious background and a keen sense of his or her responsibility to the welfare of the community.

Each family had a home with one or two bedrooms, a kitchen, a room to hang and store dried beef and sausage, and a root cellar dug into the hillside to provide storage for wine, vegetables and other perishables. For the most part farms and homes were inherited. The eldest living son inherited his parents' property. A daughter married into her ownership. Single women got jobs as a house keeper for a pastor or a widower. If a younger son married into a family that had no male heir, he often took over his in-law's farm and home. If an uncle died without heirs his property would pass to the next male who had no property. When a son inherited no one's home the entire village pitched in to build a new home and to clear forests to make new tillable fields.

By the end of the 12th century each family owned its own home and plot of land, a couple of cows, a half dozen sheep, half that many goats, a litter of pigs, and a few dozen chickens whose eggs provided a hearty breakfast and hens a plenty to make many a Sunday banquet. To be sure, the work was hard and on-going; the cows and goats had to be milked twice a day, all tasks required hard labor with primitive tools. Still, for the first time, a diligent farmer could feed his family and still have time for community-wide activities and projects with some able to indulge in leisure time.

While some decades were harder than others, life in the village did not change much from the time the first settlers arrived until this way of life vanished in the second half of the twentieth century.

Religion

There is every reason to believe that the first settlers and their descendants were religious people giving their allegiance to the Bishop of Como. For the first two hundred years they relied on traveling priests and monks to offer an occasional mass, baptize their young and provide the necessary accruements for matrimony. As the population grew, maybe to 150 people, and smaller communities began to take root in nearby settlements, the people of San Bernardo decided it was time to build a church and appeal to the good Bishop for a pastor.

In 1189, less than a century after a church was first built in Chiavenna (the largest city this side of Milan) the Bishop of Como traveled to San Bernardo to consecrate what is believed to be the second oldest church in Valchiavenna, which is a large area surrounding Chiavenna. People who had settled in the lower areas of Val San Giacomo had the advantage of more open space, income from travelers, easier access to goods, more fertile land, etc., yet it was the industrious citizens of San Bernardo who built the first church in the district. [See Addendum in Book V about Places of Worship for more information on the Church of San Bernardo.] Clearly, San

Bernardo had established itself as the leading community in Val San Giacomo.

The Prime Years [1189-1550]

There is reason to believe that life on the mountain was close to idyllic from the time the church was built until the mid-1500s. The pre-church era most likely fell into three phases. First the residents had to struggle, as described above, to clear sufficient fields, enlarge their herds, and build homes for themselves, their livestock and storage. By 1125 every family must have been comfortably situated, for the citizens would not have engaged in the arduous task of building a church unless they had more than sufficient livestock, open fields, pasture, houses and stables for every member of the community. For a few years they most likely enjoyed this relative level of affluence. This led to a desire to build a place of worship that could also serve as a community center. They may have wanted to give thanks to their God for the bounty he had provided. No doubt they wanted a place where their children could be baptized and married and they could receive the last sacraments on their death beds.

As the residents were skilled carpenters and masons, having built their own homes and stables, they could do most of the work. But to build a church they would need more. They would need to hire builders who were skilled at building a place considerably larger than their experience provided. They would need to buy a tabernacle, cruets, a chalice, statues, relics, a baptismal fount, maybe even pews and an altar. They would need the blessing of the Bishop, which meant consulting a building planner from the diocese and demonstrating they had the resources to build and then maintain a sacred place of worship. This need pushed them into the second phase, clearing more land so they could raise more sheep, goats and cows to be sold to area farmers and butchers in the valley for currency. They most likely took on more cattle from below to graze in their summer pastures, thus collecting larger fees. The entire cost of building the church had to be accumulated before laying the first stone for the foundation. Borrowing was non-existent, as the Catholic Church – and these were faithful members of the church - had outlawed usury. Even if they could have borrowed money, the congregants would have wanted the Bishop to consecrate their church on his arrival, and that meant the building had to be paid for, as the church did not allow a place of worship to be consecrated if it was indebted in any way. It is hard to believe this small group of people, maybe 150 to 200 including children, could accumulate the resources to build a church, bribe the necessary officials, pay for special indulgences, purchase permission from the central power, show a coffer large enough to sustain a pastor over time, cover the expense of a consecration, etc. in less than 20 years. It seems more reasonable that it took at least twice that time.

Once it became obvious that they were within reach of accumulating the resources, they began the last phase by cutting rocks out of the mountain and chopping down trees, especially the larch, for construction. During this period they gathered more and more native goods, hauled the things they had to purchase up the mountain, and prepared the ground where the church would sit. Stone by stone, plank by plank, beam by beam they began the laborious task of constructing a worship place for their Lord. Building the church structure itself, which had to be accomplished between the other activities of the villagers, would have taken years. The preparation of the Bishop of Como to come to consecrate the altar must have taken months. This was the biggest event in the history of the village. The Bishop of Como was the most powerful man in the Adda and Mera Valleys, ranking as a peer of the Doge of Venice. The logistics and cost of getting the Bishop from Como with his entourage had to be borne by the good congregants of San Bernardo. You can imagine the great sense of pride and relief when they gathered to say good-bye to the Bishop of Como and watched his assemblage descend down the path toward San Giacomo. Their church was built and consecrated. The parsonage was built and stocked for the pastor's comfort.

No longer needing to contribute to the building of the church, each family had more cattle than they needed for their own survival and there was the extra land that had been cleared to raise more crops during the push to build the church. There may have even been an extra house or two that they had built for the temporary workers. Suddenly the community enjoyed a sense of abundance. Their homes were their castles, their farms their salvation, and their church their comfort. This was about as good as living got for a commoner in medieval Europe.

That is not to say anyone here had the life of the noble or leisure class. They were hard working farmers to be sure, but there is no reason to believe life was particularly demanding. There was no reason to make an effort to expand; ambition need not rear its head and turn life into a struggle. All considered San Bernardo their home. This is where they were born, where they wanted to live, where they expected to die. The task was, as from the beginning, to prepare for the winter and most years in this era that was not an unduly arduous task. Now and then the people would need to build a new home for a newly married couple who were not able to move into one of their parent's homes. On rare occasion they might even have cleared a new plot as a wedding gift. With ample land, forest galore, good hunting grounds, adequate livestock, surplus of mountain grazing area, a stable population, their own parish, the people who called San Bernardo their home were content and happy.

Weddings, even more than Holy Days, were a time of community celebrations. Everyone gathered at the church for a High Mass, a lengthy sermon, a glance at the bride dressed in black, and the opportunity to rib the groom. Since everyone was related, it was more a question of how closely you were related to both the bride and the groom and how closely they were related to each other than if they were related. The ceremony was followed by a community feast – a pot-luck banquet which was followed by dancing into the wee hours of the night long after the bride and groom had snuck out to consummate their marriage.

This era was also one of political stability for San Bernardo and Val San Giacomo. Even though San Bernardo maintained minimum contact with the people living in the valley below, they were administratively and politically a part of Val San Giacomo. From 1252, Val San Giacomo had virtual autonomy, functioning as a republic with the citizens of each community electing their representatives to the Council and the council members electing the Ministrali [governor or mayor] of the area. [See the addendum in Book IV of the story of Campodolcino for detail about this system]. San Bernardo elected its representative every other year. This representative was not paid. Any property suits were settled by the council. San Bernardo had no need for a sheriff, justice system or any other political body that could have drained their coffers. The community supported the church. Maybe they paid a small fee to the Council. Other than that common expense, each family's only obligation was to support itself.

When compared to the lives of commoners in the rest of Lombardy and for that matter the rest of Europe, life on the mountain was heaven. In the neighboring Valtellina, the Franks had established a feudal system meaning that most commoners living there were now indentured. The area just beyond Chiavenna suffered from political and religious strife. This was the era of plagues, one raging through some part of Europe two or three times every century. Changes in the currents in the North Atlantic occasionally resulted in excessive rain, leading to famines that tended to wipe out huge portions of the population and turn independent farmers into beggars in the cities thereby giving the bubonic bacteria fertile grounds to multiply. The Great Plague or Black Death of 1348-1350 killed over 50% of the population of Europe and the Middle East. The farmers on San Bernardo were not immune from the weather changes and rampaging diseases, but they managed to avoid some completely and were affected less by the others. Moreover, there is no reason to believe that it was any harder to eke out an existence on the mountain than any place else in Europe. In addition to farms being periodically destroyed by war and flooding, the land everywhere had been over-farmed. Most other farmers did not have easy access to summer mountain grazing or to hunting. The open grazing land continued to provide food for the summer and the step hills provided enough drainage that the farmers managed to harvest in the severest weather. The isolation protected them from most damages of war and helped slow the spread of bacteria. There is no record that individuals either left the mountain for temporary work or migrated from the village during this era. A few women moved into their husband's homes in neighboring villages and I suppose there was the restless soul now and then that went off to Milan or Como. Yes, for four centuries San Bernardo was one of the better places in Central Europe for a commoner to live.

Ismael states at the opening of chapter 107 in *Moby Dick* that from a distant vantage point, "high abstracted man alone seems a wonder, a grandeur, a woe, but from the same point, take mankind in mass, and for the most part, they seem a mob of unnecessary duplicates, both contemporary and heredity." Paraphrasing Ismael's' observation, from my vantage point looking back, the masses of the middle ages certainly look like mobs of unnecessary duplication, while such a description would hardly be fair in describing those independent self-sufficient individuals who made San Bernardo their home.

Minor Ice Age [1550-1850]

All good things must come to an end. For the good citizens who lived on the east side of the mountain called Vergogna, the years of easy living began to abandon them as the temperatures dropped in mid-sixteenth century for the beginning of the Minor Ice Age. Winter came earlier making it harder to collect berries and chestnuts and to cure them before the first snowfall. The families needed larger supplies of food to get through the longer and fiercer winters, meaning they needed larger supplies of animal products – therefore they needed extra livestock. With longer winters, the animals needed more food and care, but the shorter summers reduced the harvest, and grass grew less abundantly on the mountainsides so the animals often did not have enough foliage to grub. There was always the need to find the delicate balance between having enough animals to provide food and not having too many that they overtaxed the land.

For the first time, the young males had to leave the mountain in the summer to seek work in the copper and rock salt mines and/or to assist along the trade route between Venice and central and northern Europe. When work was scarce, some made their way all the way to Milan and even Venice. It was about this time that the residents changed the name of the mountain they lived on from Monti di Vergogna [Mountains of Shame] to San Bernardo ai Monti [The Mountains of St. Bernard]. The change was likely motivated by the embarrassment the young encountered when seeking work.

The cold winters became more endurable when those who took jobs making wine brought home the discarded seeds, stalks, and stems that are a by-product of the winemaking process along with a recipe to make grappa. The less than tasty drink was known to warm one up and was soon the favorite drink of the farmers being forced through colder and colder winters. Eventually it took on medicinal qualities with the reputation of being able to cure anything and everything. Maybe it tasted so bad it made them forget their aches and pains.

Precipitation increased significantly in the early 1600s with the rain making it harder to plant and harvest and extreme snow on the mountains covering some of the former grazing area year round. Likewise, the mini ice age and its rains impacted the entire area which also made life harder for the people of San Bernardo. On September 4, 1618, much of Europe was shocked when the most fatal mudslide to date [only two worse since] buried the city of Piuri, a village just the other side of Chiavenna and the home of some of the most powerful traders who were central to the exchange of goods between the Orient and Central and Northern Europe. The loss of trade and the chaos created by the lack of leadership made it nearly impossible for the sons of San Bernardo residents to find work in the nearby regions of Valtellina or Valchiavenna in the ensuing decade[s].

The year 1618 also saw the beginning of the Thirty Year War [1618-1648]. The Italian Catholics living in the greater Valtellina area used the start of the conflict as an opportunity to rebel against the Protestant Grissons from Switzerland who controlled the area. They slaughtered their protestant masters calling upon themselves a harsh revenge. Because of this and the central location between the warring factions, the local populace became the pawn of the participants of the war and the victim of their complicated plots [http://encyclopedia2. thefreedictionary.com/Valtellina]. One of the most devastating wars in the history of Europe, the war was also infamous for the soldiers living off the land, taking payment from the peasants of the land they conquered by ransacking their homes and farms.

The colder weather and more rainfall brought on a severe famine that led to bread rebellions in Milan that led to further shortage of flour, bread and foodstuffs. As might be expected, as times got harder, gangs of thieves and vagabonds increased. Bravo gangs began to reign over the countryside. Laws were made threatening excessive punishments for gang members. But they flourished under the protection of this privileged class member or that – in sanctuary or at castle. This led to intensified conflict with different segments of society collaborating to protect themselves and/or attack others. As times got tougher, the Bravo gangs probably made their way to San Bernardo inflicting even more suffering on an area that was suffering from the new reality.

The Germans marched through the area in 1628 on their way to conquer Milan. They not only laid waste to the countryside, they brought with them the bubonic plague causing the devastating Italian Plague of 1629-1631 which took the lives of almost half of the citizens of Milan and over 250,000 people in Lombardy. [Read *I Promessi Sposi* – translated as *The Betrothed* – for a detail description of this era in the greater Milan valley]. Aware the German army was marching their way, many local residents who lived in the valley headed toward the mountains and there is no reason to believe that San Bernardo failed to welcome them. Luckily, they came before the Germans brought the bubonic bacteria with them and San Bernardo escaped any direct devastation from the Plague. They certainly suffered from the side effects, not the least of which was the people again took on the burden of building a church to honor San Rocco whom they credited with saving their community from the effects of the Italian Plague. [See addendum in Book V on The Churches for the story of the origins of San Rocco Chapel.] In order to avoid infection, conscription, and the effects of the war, the boys of San Bernardo stayed put for the years the plague and war raged. Even if they had dared to join the raucous, the economy of the Padana region was so devastated there was little opportunity for citizens coming off the mountain to find work.

During this period, Val San Giacomo maintained its relative independence. True, they were under the rule of the Grisons, but they were able to stay out of the thirty year war. San Bernardo, isolated as it was, completely avoided the direct consequences. There is no record of the famine or plague taking the lives of San Bernardo residents indicating that they found a way to share their meager resources. The people of San Bernardo kept their boys close to home to avoid the conflicts and diseases the outside soldiers brought with them. Even with reduced resources, never before were they so happy to be hidden on the mountainside.

By mid-century, the area settled down. The punishing weather continued, but the youth of San Bernardo filled the gap with supplies bought in from their work in the salt and copper mines, the fields in Ticino and Grison and in the cities of Chiavenna, Milan and Venice. A significant change in diet had a huge impact on the health of the residents. The potato was introduced to Europe from the Native Americans and made its way to San Bernardo. The potato had a short growing season, stored easily and for long periods in a root cellar and was packed full of vitamins that had not been in the mostly meat and milk diet. Although life was significantly harder than it had been for the previous four centuries, life on the mountain had to have been better than what the commoner suffered in the lowlands during this era when life was difficult and guarded and every man had to watch out for himself.

Alessandro Manzoni describes this phenomenon concisely in *I Promessi Sposi*:

> The man who is ready to give and expecting to receive offense every moment, naturally seeks allies and companions. Hence the tendency of individuals to unite into classes was in these times carried to the greatest excess; new societies were formed, and each man strove to increase the power of his own party to the greatest degree. The clergy were on the watch to defend and extend their immunities; the nobility their privileges, the military their exemptions. Tradespeople and artisans were enrolled in subordinate confraternities; lawyers constituted a league, and even doctors a corporation. Each of these little oligarchies had its own peculiar authority and vigor, of the united force of the many. Honest men availed themselves of this advantage for defense; the evil-disposed and sharp-witted made use of it to accomplish deeds of violence, for which their personal means were insufficient, and to insure themselves of impunity.

> *-The Betrothed*, p11

There is no reason to believe the citizens of San Bernardo submitted to these enemies or paranoia.

Revolutions racked Europe during the fourth quarter of the eighteenth century. Tired of the off and on again conflicts between Spain, France, Venice and Milan, the Council of Val San Giacomo sought from time to time to have the Grisons annex them as a fourth district. In September of 1797, fearing an invasion by the French, the Grisons finally moved to combine forces with Val San Giacomo as a fourth district of their canton. But it was too late. In fact, many citizens from the valley and beyond welcomed the French invasion under Napoleon as liberators from the Austrians who had demanded allegiance for the past 150 years. In October, Commissioner Aldini conceded the area to the new Cisalpine state set up by Napoleon with its headquarters in Milan. For the next 18 years [except for an eleven month interlude in 1789-1800], the French ruled the area. On the downside, Napoleon took away the independence that Chiavenna and Val San Giacomo had maintained for the better part of seven centuries by making the area part of the Cisalpine Republic in 1797 and part of the Kingdom of Italy in 1805. The loss of independence was accompanied by tighter security and the area became a safer place to live. In 1815, the Austrians took back control and created the Kingdom of Lombardy/Venice and Val San Giacomo, including San Bernardo, was annexed to the new kingdom. On May 1, 1816 Val San Giacomo was divided into three political units and each unit divided into four wards. San Bernardo was one of the four wards that belonged to the outer terziere that was headquartered in the village of San Giacomo.

Life was no bed of roses on the mountain during these three centuries; still, life must have been relatively good, because there is no record of any mass migration off the mountain during this period. It seems that the young men were not tempted to relocate to other communities indicating that life was probably better on the mountain than the places where they found temporary employment. The population remained relatively stable in San Bernardo, while places like Milan were from time to time halved by war and disease.

Life on San Bernardo ai Monti 1848-1918

From 1815 to 1848, the area was controlled by the Austrians who returned political stability. In this period, the summers got longer and the winters milder. The longer seasons assured more plentiful grazing in the pastures and larger crops off the fields. The longer days provided more opportunity to clear more forests. The shorter winters demanded less feed for the animals, firewood for the houses, grappa for the men and spinning for the women. There was reason to think that life on the mountain would get easier.

Along with warmer weather, political stability, more leisure time, improved nutritional food [polenta made from corn became a staple and, along with the potato, provided valuable balance to the local diet], and advances in medicine contributing to better understandings of diseases and their prevention, came more births and longer lives. In the direct ancestry of the Pedretti family, Guglielmo Pedretti [1804-1869] and Teresa Cerletti [1805-1853] had 15 children with the average life span of 47 years [one lived past 80]. Guglielmo and his siblings only averaged a life span of 27 years with the longest-living barely reaching the age of 65. Guglielmo's father [1753-1797] and his siblings only managed to average 14 years each with his father the only one to live past 24 [he died at 44]. While this is only one case study, the tendency to have larger families, and for the members of each new generation to live significantly longer than the previous generation, led to population explosion and the lands of San Bernardo could no longer support the populace.

Starting around 1800 more and more inhabitants [as well as those living in similar places] were forced to get jobs in the copper and rock salt mines, to seek jobs in Chiavenna which, of course, became scarcer leading to the sons of San Bernardo traveling to Milan, Venice and even Rome for work. Others headed in the other direction and sought jobs in Ticino and Grison Cantons in Switzerland. It is very possible that Stefano Pedretti who had gained the nickname of "Camoscin" spent one or more summers raising and harvesting grain in a village over 200 kilometers northwest called Airolo which was the bread basket of the Levantine valley of the Canton Ticino. There he may have met his bride to be, Adelaide Lombardi, who was of the upper crust of that community. More and more of the people who left the mountain to earn resources to keep San Bernardo residents alive during the winters decided it made more sense to permanently relocate. Youth from San Bernardo moved to Chiavenna, Milan, Venice, Rome and Locarno in search of new lives. The growing impact of the industrial revolution opened up jobs not only in factories and mines, but also to build roads and to work the fields that the former serfs had left to man the machines in the factories. In the 1840s residents from Val San Giacomo began to migrate to the United States of America. Several made their way to work in the lead mines near Galena, Illinois. When the area along the Mississippi north of Galena opened up for settlers, Giuseppe Monti, Augustine Zaboglio and others hatched the idea to resettle there to set up a center of trade and farming. After they had selected and settled the bucolic area in Wisconsin now called Genoa, they sent word back to Campodolcino and Airolo that there was opportunity a plenty with plats of 40 acres for sale by the government for next to nothing.

Meanwhile a popular uprising [1848-49] in Lombardy temporarily forced the Austrians out. On May 29, 1849, over 561,000 people from Lombardy voted to unite under Italian rule while less than 700 voted against the referendum. But internal conflicts and a lack of trust between peasants and the privileged class led to victory for the Austrians, and the territory again fell into their hands. Defeated in their efforts to break free of the Austrians and suffering from another famine, the ravages of war, over population, over-worked farm land and little hope for a brighter future at home, more and more people looked to America for salvation. In the next decade, close to forty families, including the three oldest sons of Guglielmo Pedretti and Teresa Cerletti, from the Campodolcino area made their way to Genoa, Wisconsin.

The population in San Bernardo peaked in the mid-nineteenth century with a little over 300 people in permanent residence. For the next seventy years, the population was stable with enough people emigrating to arrest further over-population. Those that stayed enjoyed the benefits of a tightknit community, a strong and supportive religious environment, textbook security, adequate leisure time, serene and uncompromising beauty, and a genuine sense of community. San Bernardo was home in the warmest and most comforting meaning of that word. Those that left found adventure, hope for a better future and for some, wealth and comfort beyond anything they could even imagine before they left. Just the same, more than a few returned to their home in the mountain for their twilight years.

Once Italy became a unified country [1861], it became easier for the young people to relocate within the country's borders. While some residents continued to immigrate to the Americas, most found their way to Milan, Venice, and Rome as well as many other communities. Today Italians who can trace their roots back to San Bernardo are spread throughout the Peninsula.

San Bernardo Today [1918-2012]

Let's jump forward to 1945. World War II is over. Italy needs to rebuild and opportunities abound in Chiavenna, Milan, Venice and Rome. The young men coming back from the war have seen places, not as beautiful as San Bernardo to be sure, but far more bountiful and less harsh. Throughout Europe, floods are now controlled by dams, pestilence by advances in medicine, thieves are not strangers but they no longer control the countryside, democracy has blunted the dominance of the privileged class, and the new economy offers opportunities to the ambitious and talented.

In the 1920s a cable rail had been built by a private electric company. An electric generator had been erected just below the village and the homes were wired for electricity. For a time, this must have seemed to have been heaven sent. The residents could live in their haven, but have easier access to the bounty below. Problem was, it was no longer any safer from outside dangers than any other place and the young saw how much easier life elsewhere could be. So instead of strengthening the community, the original advantages of mountain living dissolved and the people were left with barren, steep land, harsh winters, and a decreasing population. Equally important, new means of travel and communication had denied the mountain village its once-prized isolation resulting in the sons of San Bernardo families being conscripted to fight Mussolini's war.

Modernization turned out to be a curse, not only for the traditional way of life but, for the very existence of the village. The community and the area began to thin out between 1918 and 1946. After WW II, the number of residents who "migrated downstream" to Chiavenna, Milan, and places far and wide increased rapidly. During the 1950s, they abandoned the village with a vengeance. In the 1970s, when a road was built connecting San Bernardo to San Giacomo and from there the rest of the world, some residents felt the community might again become the home of year-round residents interested in harvesting the forest, tilling the land and breeding animals. That did not happen. Instead, goats and sheep become as scarce as a fresh piece of flat land, the few chickens seemed to run wild and soon there was not a cow or pig to be seen anywhere, and the trees reclaimed vast portions of the mountainside. Those who still breed animals today are "gentleman farmers" raising a few sheep and goats as a diversion from how they make a living elsewhere. More than half the land once tilled has returned to forest as it had been a thousand years ago.

Nonetheless, the lure of the air, the palliative panorama, and the soothing memories of growing up in a place as close to heaven as can be found, attracted the people back and they began to modernize their family homes. Today San Bernardo is a vibrant vacation community made up of 500 or so descendants of former residents and others who have discovered the serenity, harmony and sense of community that come with the stunning vistas in every direction and the clarity of the sky on a clear night. Alberto Cerletti, born and raised in San Bernardo and himself a "holiday" resident, noted to me, "Now the residents living throughout the year are a dozen. S. Bernardo has become a holiday village, and in fact at the weekends, for the Christmas holidays, Easter and the summer holidays, many people come back. San Bernardo has never lost the affection of its original descendants and has won new admirers, who just come to breathe the fresh air, peace and tranquility that this lovely country has to offer in all seasons of the year."

There is no day that more people come back than on August 15 when the village is flooded with former residents back for the annual "Reunion" held on The Feast of the Assumption at the church of San Bernardo. Five hundred people enjoy a traditional lunch made from local produce; there are games to play, activities for all but, most importantly, many friends to enjoy and with whom to reminisce.

While its purpose has changed, the village maintains a sense of self. The town makes no effort to be what it isn't. When I visited, I witnessed no yearning for the agricultural subsistence of yesterday or the selling out to the tourist of tomorrow. I felt welcomed and at home in a place that now serves as home to seasonal residents. The people here know who they are, why they are here and what they want from their community.

PostScript: Today's descendants of the original settlers of San Bernardo are kind and gentle. They do not step on their neighbor to get ahead. No one is a better friend in time of need. Most are fiercely independent and self-reliant. They are strong and many could be called workaholics. Therefore I think it reasonable to conjecture that the original settlers of San Bernardo, who arrived around 850, wanted control over their own destiny and were sick and tired of avarice, violence and submission. As the members of the village tended to marry inside their own ranks, it is also likely that anyone whose origin goes back to San Bernardo, including the Genoa Pedretti family, could trace their ancestry back to these original pioneers.

An empty cistern in August 2009

The first trough provided water for drinking and cooking. The second trough was used to rinse clothes and other items they had cleaned in the bottom trough.

Spindle used to tie bundles of hay and rye

Remnants of two-story stable that once belonged to the Cerletti family in Selene. Top story was used for hay and the lower story was where the livestock lived in the winter. The stable is attached to neighbor's house which is seen off to the right. The roof of the Cerletti's pig and/ or chicken pen can be seen at ground level to the right of picture. Picture is taken from in front of Cerletti home.

San Bernardo Church covered with snow during a recent winter.
During the "Minor Ice Age" the snowfalls were much larger.

Building where electricity was generated can be seen at the left of picture

ADDENDUM C

Pedigree Chart

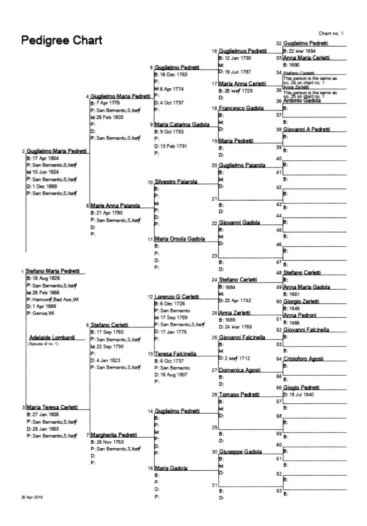

Pedigree Chart

Chart no. 1

Some of the Children

Stephen	Dale Charles	Cathy	Tammy Lynn	Daniel	Ryan Paul
Joseph	Ruth	Dennis	Andrew Phillip	Tami Marie	Beth Lou
William	James	Angie	Dale	Dale	Valerie
Peter	John	Helen Marie	Randy	Michael	Timothy J
Alois	Jean Ann	Janet	Diane	Susan	Carrie Ann
Albert	Harlan Thomas	Theresa Marie	Doreen Joan	Kay Marie	Vicki Kay
Victor	Richard	John D.	Jerome	John David	Patrick John
Paul	Patricia A	Susan Kay	Marilyn	Lisa	John
Mary Margaret	Robert	Kay Marie	Michelle	Mark	Wayne Francis
Margaret May	Leo Maurus	Barbara Jean	Rosemary Kay	Robert Arthur	Denise Linda
Ada Therese	Mary Agnes	Richard Carl	Mark Francis	Gregory	Robert
Agnes	David Paul	Mark	Terri T.	Lara	Kevin Thomas
Alvin	Elaine	Carole Florence	Timmy	Amy Marie	Tara Lynn
Anna Mae	Charles Phillip	Jackie L.	Cindy	Charles	Melissa
Carl	Douglas	Donnie	Infant	Jon Paul	Laura Michelle
Carol Marie	Dennis	Ann Marie	Thomas	Kenneth James	Roxanne Marie
Clara Helen	Linda	Gary	Robert	Leann	Ryan Royce
Francis W.	Shirley Ann	Mary Ann	Edward	Jon Ralph	Jennifer
Bernard	Russel	Betty Lou	Linda	Tricia Renee	Michael
Lawrence	Terry Richard	Tracy	Robert T	Thomas	Andrea
Raymond	Herman Jr.	Michael	William	Christine	Nicole
Marie Helen	James	Julie Jo	Catherine	Judy	Amanda
Dolores Monica	Story	Jane	Bruce Clifford	Gary Linder	David
Marvin Levi	Gary Charles	Thomas W.	Janet Marie	Tony Richard	Becki Lynn
Lucille Marie	Vernon	Anthony	Jill	Ted Joseph	Ryan Michael
Joseph Peter	Karen	Christine	Sonja Louise	Donna Sue	Marie
No Name	Michael Peter	Dorothy Mae	Susan Marie	Stephanie Jean	Heidi
Margaret Mary	Paul Anthony	Linda Ann	Kelly Jean	Ann Marie	Heather R
Donald Victor	Joseph	Randy	Edward	Richard	Mark Allen
James Albert	Linda Ann	Steve	Lori Ann	Jennifer Marie	Jason Patrick
Ralph Paul	Don Bernard	Deborah	Corinne Marie	Troy David	Jessica
Joan Cecilia	Karen Marie	Sharon	Jill M.	Andrew	Jennifer
Therese	Edward	Gary	Mark	Brian	Eric
Marilyn	Richard David	Rick	Raymond	James	Richard
Shirley Jeanne	Catherine	James Victor	Dean	Jodi Ann	Thomas Walter
Rita	Thomas Allen	Allan Paul	Todd Arnold	Michelle	Jill Marie
James Victor	Bonnie	James E.	Kelly	Dawn	Cyndi Kathleen
William	Mary Jo	Jerome Donald	Tracy	Teresa Diane	Gregory
Francis Gerald	Larry Anthony	Lisa	Alice	Mark	Laura Ann
Ronald Joseph	Sandra	Peter Gregory	Margery Ann	Jennifer Ann	Victoria Jean
Geraldine Ann	Trudy	Jody	Lisa Marie	Gary	Mark Patrick
Duane Joseph	Dennis John	Susan	Karen Marie	S Kay	John
Arnold Richard	Jaynne	Kathleen Marie	Raymond John	Aimee Beth	Staci Jean
Robert Francis	Patrick Daniel	Gina	Anthony	Tricia Ann	Anthony Paul
Mary Jane	Kathy	Cheryl	Ricardo	Leanne	Steven
Edward Peter	Rose Ann	Frank Joseph	Trent Thomas	Timothy John	Lee Gehard
Kenneth	Randy	Roger	Lisa Ann	Michael Jerome	Timothy
Donna Mae	Stanley Steven	Mary Jo	Sharon	Scott	Heidi
Berneal M	Jean	Robert	Mary	Michele Marie	Rebecca
Thomas	Anne Margaret	William	Anthony	April Ann	Anna Mae
Patrick	Kim Terese	Janet M.	Patrick	Jennifer Ann	Michael
Daniel Gregory	Mary Ann	Steven Francis	Perry	Susan Ann	Amanda
Mary Lee	Vicki	Julie	Emily	Todd Glenn	Victoria
Dorothy Lee	Donna	Carol	Paula Anne	Kari Marie	
Gerald	Barbara	Jeffrey Jon	Kevin Ronald	Shari	
Earl	Jeanne Marie	Barbara	Joseph	Tonya Jeanne	
Michael Arthur	Monica Ann	Russell	Julie Marie	Anthony	
Jerome "Jerry"	Kathy Anne	Karen Lee	Debra Lynn	Bridget Leigh	

ADDENDUM D

Primary Documents

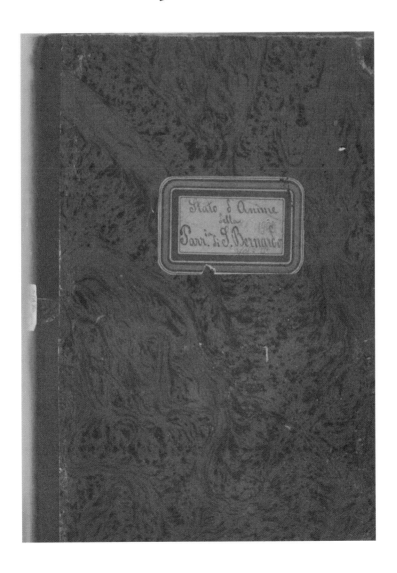

Anno IX - n. 10 - OTTOBRE 1989

UN COGNOME ALLA VOLTA
a cura di Remo Bracchi e Francesco Palazzi Trivelli

PEDRETTI - Questo ceppo è derivato da quello dei Gadòla. Già il 6 ottobre 1531 in un atto di Vincenzo Oldradi presenzia come testimone Guglielmo di Pietro dela Gadola, nominato Guglielmo fu Pietro detto Pedretto dela Gadola dei Monti di San Bernardo in un atto del 13 febbraio 1563, steso dal notaio Isacco Lupi. Da quest'ultimo sappiamo di un livello concesso a Giovanni e Guglielmo fu Pedretto dela Gadola il 23 gennaio 1559. Tre atti del 1596 del notaio Paolo Peverelli ci danno la nuova forma cognominale "del Pedretto": Giovanni fu Antonio del Pedretto della Gadola, teste il 5 maggio, Cristoforo fu Guglielmo del Pedretto della Gadola, confinante il 3 dicembre, mentre il 30 marzo avevamo incontrato un Guglielmo fu Giovanni del Pedretto della Gadola dei Monti di San Bernardo, ma abitante a Monastero di Samolaco e padre di Cipriano e Maria, nati dalla fu Anastasia Sturnoni di Monastero. Nel secolo successivo troviamo la forma moderna del cognome: Silvestro fu Cristoforo Pedretti, teste l'8 gennaio 1641.

Alcuni Pedretti si portarono anche a Chiavenna, come un Giovanni Domenico Pedretti fu Giovanni di Gordona, teste il 30 dicembre 1744 e che ignoriamo se appartenesse allo stesso ceppo di San Bernardo, mentre era sposa a uno di costoro, Pietro Alberto Pedretti fu Pietro di Val San Giacomo, abitante a Chiavenna, una signora Marta fu Carlo Maranese di Chiavenna.

Stemmi dei Pedretti sono in pietra dipinta sotto il portico di San Lorenzo e in stucco dipinto sopra un portale al piano nobile di palazzo Pedretti appunto, in via Dolzino 21 a Chiavenna, oggi proprietà Scaramellini.

Il cognome Pedretti è di origine patronimica, significando figlio di Pietro, qui nella forma dialattale Pedro, con suffisso diminutivo -etto. Quando nella famiglia si ripeteva lo stesso nome da padre in figlio, per distinguere l'uno dall'altro si usavano formazioni diminutive: Pedro, Pedretto, Pedrettino.

Le notizie sono tratte dall'Archivio di Stato di Sondrio, Notarile, volumi 1006, 1542, 1837, 5099.

Article claiming first San Bernardo person using the name Pedretti was 6 October 1531

VN COGNOME ALLA VOLTA
a cura di Remo Bracchi e Francesco Palazzi Trivelli

Valchiavenna

monthly

information, sport and culture

Year IX – n. 10 - 10 October 1989

PEDRETTI – The Pedretti family name is derived from Gadòla. As early as October 6, 1531 an act of Vincenzo Oldradi was witnessed by William the son of Pietro dela Gadola. In a deed written by the notary Isaac Lupi and dated February 13, 1563, William son of Peter called Pedretto of Gadola from San Bernardo Mountain is cited. From Lupi we know of a privilege granted on January 23, 1559 to Giovanni (John) and Guglielmo (William) to use the surname Pedretto of the house of Gadola. Three documents from 1596 by the notary Paolo Peverelli use the new surname "del Pedretto" - Giovanni son of Antonio del Pedretto della Gadola, testified on May 5; Cristoforo son of William Pedretto of Gadola was cited on December 3; while on March 30 Pevereilli wrote that he had met William, son of Giovanni Pedretto della Gadola from Mt. San Bernardo, who was an inhabitant of the Monastery of Samolaco and the guardian for Cipriano and Maria, born to Anastasia Sturnoni of the Monastery. The following century we find the modern form of the surname: Silvestro the son of Cristoforo Pedretti witnessed a document on January 8, 1641.

Some Pedrettis also moved to Chiavenna, such as Giovanni Domenico Pedretti the son of Giovanni of Gordon was a witness on December 30, 1744 and we should not ignore that Pietro Alberto Pedretti, of the same San Bernardo tree, was living in Chiavenna and was married to Miss Marta, daughter of Carlo Maranese of Chiavenna.

The Pedretti coat of arms is painted on stone at Portico di San Lorenzo and on stucco over a portal on the main floor of Pedretti Palace, via Dolzino 21 in Chiavenna - today the property of Scaramellini.

The surname Pedretti is of patronymic origin, meaning son of Peter, here in the vernacular form Pedro, with diminutive suffix-etto. When the same name was repeated in the family from father to son, diminutive formations were used to distinguish one from the other: Pedro, Pedretto, Pedrettino.

The information is from the State Archives of Sondrio, Notary, volumes 1006, 1542, 1837, and 5099

Following is a selection of facsimiles of the records held at San Bernardo Church in San Bernardo that were used to trace the ancestry of Stefano Maria Pedretti. Also included are the birth and death certificates of his spouse and copies of records found that were used to identify his children. The translations provided are close approximations of what is written in the documents that were composed mostly in Latin but sometimes interspersed with local dialect.

Book Cover

Records of Marriages for San Bernardo Church

Beginning with 1685

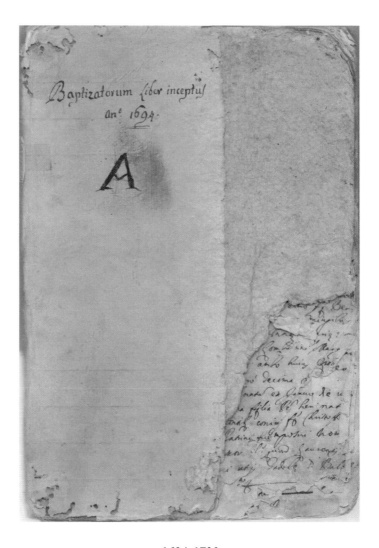

1694-1730
Book of Baptisms
San Bernardo Church

Baptism of Lorenzo Giuseppe Cerletti (born december, 8 1725)

In the year of Jesus thousand seven-hundred twenty-five day eight of the
month of December, Very Reverend Mr Francesco Cerletti, had the consent
by Giovanni Pietro Signorelli vice-parson of the church of S.Bernardo ai
Monti, committee of Chiavenna dioceses of Como, baptizes the infant, born
in the day six in the same month, by Stefano Cerletti and Anna Cerletti
daughter of Giorgio called "del Lorenzo", spouses. The name given is
Lorenzo Giuseppe The godparents are: Giorgio Dell'Agosto son of Giacomo
and Maria Musciatti daugther of Battista everybody of this parish.

Baptismal record of Lorenzo Giuseppe Cerletti
[born 6 Dec. 1725]

In the year one thousand and seven hundred and twenty
five on the eighth day of December, the Very Reverend Francesco
Cerletti-having the consent of Giovani Pietro Signorelli, the
vice-parson of the Church of Mt. San Bernardo and committee
of Chiavenna part of the dioceses of Como, baptized the infant,
born in the sixth day of the same month to Stefano Cerletti
and Anna Cerletti daughter of Giorgio called, "del Lorenzo";
spouses. The name given is Lorenzo Giuseppe. The godparents
are Giorgio Dell'Agosto, son of Giacomo and Maria Musciatti,
daughter of Battista. Everyone is from this parish.

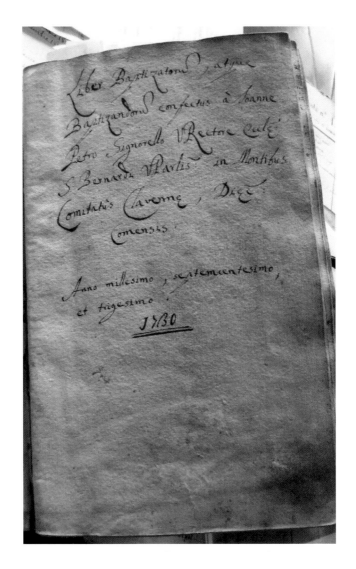

1730 - 1815

Book Cover

The Book of Baptisms for San Bernardo Church

17 September 1759
Record of marriage of
Laurentius G. Cerletti and Theresia Falcinelle

In the year one thousand seven-hundred and fifty-nine on the seventeenth day of September omitted publications arrived granting permission of the Most Illustrious Vicar General and Executor Apostolic of Diocese of Como, Bishop Giovanni Battista Peregrino Epifania dated the seventh day of August. Not having identified impediments, I, Doctor in Sacred Theology, Notary for Apostolic Authority and Parson of this church of Mt. San Bernardo, San Giacomo Valley, a member of Chiavenna district in the dioceses of Como, Cristofaro Lombardini, present Lorenzo son of Stefano Cerletti and Teresa daughter of Giovanni Falcinella and had their consent, I have solemnly joined in marriage, and I have blessed them according to the rite of Holy Roman Church.

Present witnesses known and popular: Antonio son of Tommaso Lombardini - Notary, Lorenzo son of "Ministrale" Pietro Pedretti and Silvestro son of Tommaso Lombardini - Notary.

All people cited are from the parish of S Bernardo.

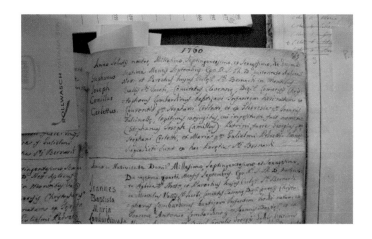

17 September 1760
Baptismal Record of Stephanus Joseph Camillus Cerletti

6 April 1775
Baptismal Record of Guglielmo Maria Pedretti

Anno dei millesimo, septingentesimo, septuages-
imo Quinto die septima Mensis Aprilis ego P.S. Th. D.
Christophoris Lombardinis parochis husis eccle St Bernardi,
comitatis Clavenne, Comensis baptizavi, infantem heri natiom
ex Guglielmo f. Pedretti, et ex Cattharina f. Francifis Gadola,
coniuqibis hesus parochie St. Bernrdi, cui impositum, fuit
nomen Gulielmus maria Latrini fuere gulielmes f. q Aiterey
Pedretti et Dominica f. Francisci Gadole ambo ex hoc parochia

In the year of one thousand and seven hundred and sev-
enty-five on day seven of the month of April, I, Christopher
Lombardini, doctor of sacred theology, notary for apostolic
authority, and pastor of this church of S. Bernardo a member
of Chiavenna, of the dioceses of Como, baptized the infant
born yesterday to Guglielmo, son of Guglielmo Pedretti and
to Caterina the daughter of Francesco Gadola, spouses of this
parish of S. Bernardo.

Baptismal Record
Anna Mara Paiarola
April 21, 1780

In the year one thousand seven-hundred and eighty on the twenty first day of April, I Giovanni Battista Buzetti, pastor of this church of San Bernardo, in of Chiavenna district of the dioceses of Como, baptize the infant born in this night to Silvestro, son of Guglimo Paiarola and Maria Orsola, daughter of consul Giovanni Gadola, legitimate spouses of this parish. The name given is Anna Maria. The godparents are Guglielmo, son of Giovani Barini and Teresa, daughter of Lieutenant Guglielmo Lombardini, wife of Giovani Lombardini. All are from the parish of San Bernardo.

Book II Cover
Records of Marriages for San Bernardo Parish
In the Valley of St. James by Pastor John Baptist Buzzetti
Beginning in the year 1787

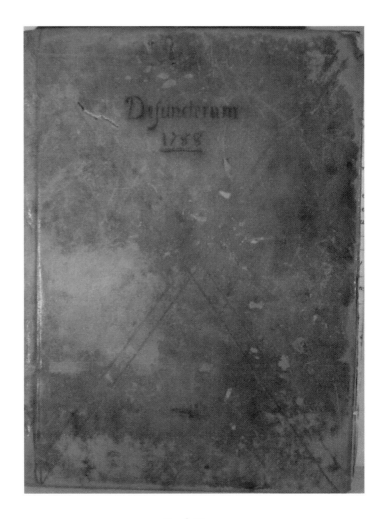

Book Cover
Records of Deaths for San Bernardo Church
Beginning in 1788

Marriage record for Stefano Cerletti and Margherita Pedretti
22 Sept 1790

In the year one thousand and seven hundred and ninety on the 22nd day of September, having omitted the regular publications as a result from the document of the 4th day of September granted by the Reverend Don Geronimo Stoppini, vicar, that there isn't any obstacle; I, Reverend Giovanni Battista Buzetti of this church of S. Bernardo and on this altar asked Stefano son of Lorenzo Cerletti and Margarita daughter of Guglielmo Pedretti both of this parish of S. Bernardo and they gave their solemn consent of marriage.

Witnesses of the marriage are Pietro Geronimi son of Guglielmo, Giuseppe Pedretti son of Guglielmo and Giovanni Cerletti son of Lorenzo – all are from the parish of S. Bernardo.

I blessed them according to the rite of the Holy Roman Church.

Marriage of Guglielmo Pedretti and Maria Ann Paiarola (1803)

In the year one thousand and eight hundred and three, omitted the usual publications, as a result from the document of the 9th day of May; it was granted by the Reverand Claudio Riva, general vicar, and emerged an impediment of consanguinity of 4th degree of both families of Guglielmo Pedretti and of Maria Anna daughter of Silvestro Paiarola, both of the parish of San Bernardo Obtained for them the exoneration certificate, from the Apostolic See and dispense from the authority by the illustrious Rev. Fiar Carlo Rovelli of the order of preachers Bishop of Como and in this dossier Apostolic performer on the ninth day of the month of May.

No obstacle found, I, father Giovanni Battista Buzzetti, parson of this church of San Bernardo, in front of this main altar, I asked them, I obtained their mutual consent and I joined them in marriage. Present witnesses known and suitable Father Giovanni Valentino, Rotmund of San Rocco, Minestrale Giovanni Cerletti son of Lorenzo and Guglielmo Barii son of Giovanni. After celebration of mass there is a blessing according to the right of holy Roman Church.

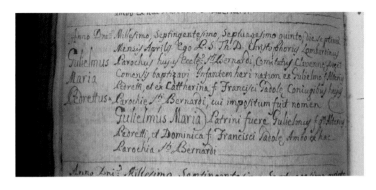

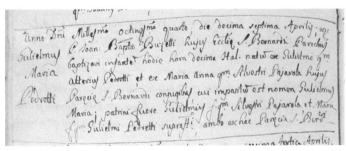

Baptismal records of Guglielmo Maria Pedretti
(born 17 April 1804)

In the year one-thousand and eight hundred and four on day seventeen of April, I, Parson Giovani Battista Buzzetti, pastor of the parish of San Bernardo baptize the infant born today at ten o'clock to Guglielmo the son of Guglielmo Pedretti and to Maria Anna the daughter of Silvestro Paiarola, spouses of this parish of San Bernardo. The name given to the child is Guglielmo Maria. The godparents are Guglielmo Paiarola the son of Silvestro and Maria Pedretti daughter of Guglielmo. All are members of the parish of S. Bernardo.

Baptismal record of Mara Teresa Cerletti
(Born 27 January 1805)

In the year of one-thousand eight-hundred and five on the twenty-seventh day of January, I Giovanni Battista Buzzetti, pastor of San Bernardo on the twenty-eighth of January baptize the infant born approximately at eleven o'clock on the twenty-seventh to Stefano the son of Lorenzo Cerletti and Margherita the daughter of Guglielmo Pedretti, spouses of this parish of San Bernardo. The name given is Maria Teresa. The godparents are Giovanni the son of Giovani Gadola and Maria the daughter of Antonio Lombardi son of Silvestro. All are from this parish of San Bernardo.

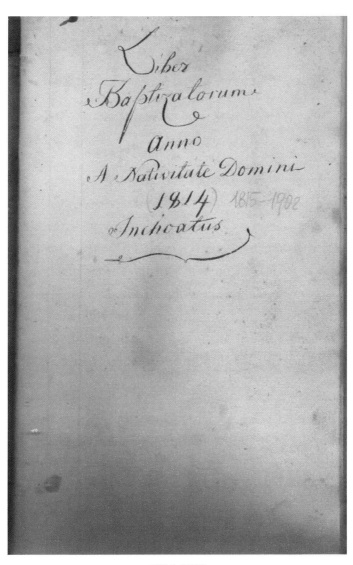

1814-1902

Book Cover

Records of Baptisms for San Bernardo Church

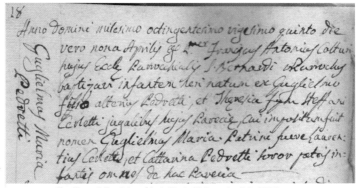

Baptism of Guglielmo Maria Pedretti (born April 9, 1825)

In the year of Jesus thousand eight-hundred and twenty-five, day nine of April, I parson Francesco Antonio Colturi, parson of this parish of San Bernardo, baptizes the infant born yesterday by Guglielmo son of Guglielmo Pedretti and Teresa daughter of Stefano Cerletti both of this parish, the name given is Guglielmo Maria. The godparents are Lorenzo Cerletti and Caterina Pedretti sister of the father of the infant, everybody of this parish.

In the year one thousand and eight-hundred and twenty-five on the ninth day of April, I reverend Francesco Antonio Colturi, pastor of this parish of St. Bernard, baptize the infant born yesterday to Guglielmo son of Guglielmo Pedretti and Teresa, daughter of Stefano Cerletti, both members of this church, who is given the name Guglielmo Maria. The godparents are Lorenzo Cerletti and Caterina Pedretti sister of the father of the infant. All are members of this parish.

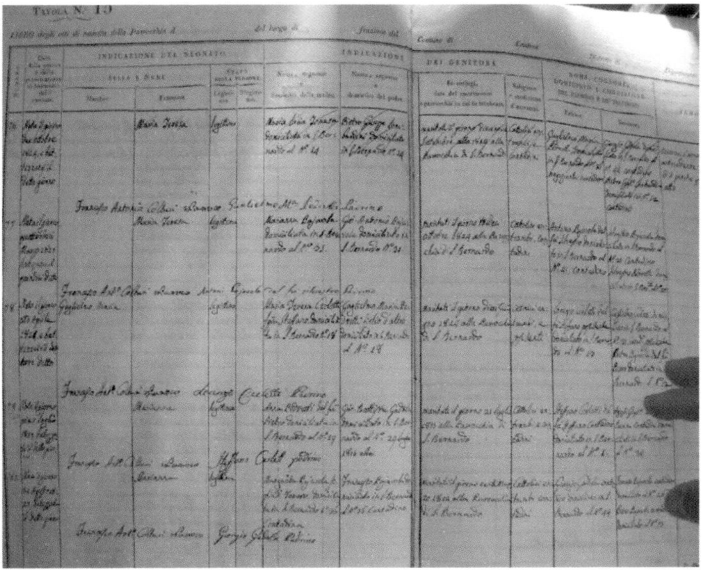

Date of birth and of presentation for baptism	Name	State of person	Name of mother	Name of father	Marriage of parents	Religion	Name of godfather	Witnesses
Born on April 8, 1825 and baptized on the same day	Guglielmo Maria	legitimate	Maria Teresa Cerletti, daughter of Stefano Who lives in San Bernardo No. 18	Guglielmo Maria Pedretti son of person with same name who lives in San Bernardo No. 18	They were married on June 10, 1824 in the church of San Bernardo	Catholic	Lorenzo Cerletti of Stefano, xxx lives in San Bernardo at K 13	Guglielmo Cerletti who lives in San Bernardo at 21

Birth Certificate
Notation in Tavola No. 15
Guglielmo Maria Pedretti

Baptism of Stefano Maria Pedretti (born August 15, 1826)

In the year of Jesus thousand eight-hundred twenty-six , day fifteen of the month of August, I, Parson Francesco Antonio Colturi, baptize the infant born today, son of Guglielmo Maria Pedretti son of another Guglielmo called "Guglielmone", and Teresa Cerletti daughter of Stefano, spouses. The name given is Stefano Maria. The godparents are Stefano Cerletti son of another Stefano and Maria Orsola Pedretti daughter of the cited Guglielmo.

They named the baby Silvestro Maria. Godparents are Silvestro Pedretti son of the above mentioned Guglielmo and Maria Cerletti the daughter of Stefano

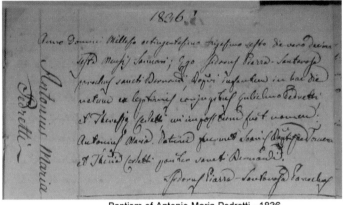

Baptism of Antonio Maria Pedretti - 1836

In the year one thousand and eighteen and thirty-six on the 13th day of February, I Isidoro Piazza Santarosa, pastor of S. Bernardo, baptize the infant born today to the legitimate spouses Guglielmo Pedretti and Teresa Cerletti, who gave the child the name Antonio Maria. The godparents are Giovanni Battista Tomera and Teresa Cerletti.

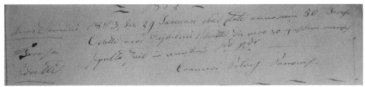

Teresa Cerletti – died in 29 January 1853

In the year 1853 on the 29th day of January, Teresa Cerletti, wife of Guglielmo Pedretti died at age 50. She was buried on the 30th day of the month in S. Bernardo cemetery. Signed Pietro Crameri -Pastor

Guglielmo Maria Pedretti – died 1 December 1869

Guglielmo Maria Pedretti: In the year 1869 on first day of December he died. With the usual ritual of the Catholic Church Guglielmo Pedretti was buried in the cemetery of S. Bernardo on the second day of the month cited. He was 65 years old. His father was Guglielmo Pedretti and his mother Mariana Paiarola. –Pietro Crameri, pastor

The Book of Births
Teresa Pedretti plus six siblings

Tavola n. 15

Libro degli atti di nascita dela Parrocchia di [San Bernardi] del luogo di [Salina]

Anno, mese, giorno ed ora della nascita, e giorna della presenlazione del neonato al batlesimo

Indicazione Del Neonato

Susso e nomine maschio femmina

Stato della persona

Legittimo illegettimo

Nome, cognomen e domicilio della madre

Nome, cognomen e domicilio della padre

Salina

Pedretti Teresa fu Guglielmo e fu Teresa Cerletti nata 1840,
 19, Febbraio

Caterina, sorelle fu Guglielmo e fu Teresa Cerletti nata 1843,
 14 Novembre

Maria sorelle fu Guglielmo e fu Teresa Cerletti nata 1845, 17 Gennaio

Francesco fratello fu Guglielmo e fu Teresa Cerletti nata 1847, 19,
 Decembre Maritato in America

Guglielmo fratello fu Guglielmo e fu Teresa Cerletti nata 1825, 8
 Aprile Chili

Silvestro fratello fu Guglielmo e fu Teresa Cerletti nata 1827 10
 Novembre America Mort oil 4 Decembre 1875 in America

Bernardo fratello fu Guglielmo e fu Teresa Cerletti nata 1834, 1
 Gennaio Zurigo marita

TABLE NUMBER 15 [Translation by Michael Pedretti]

The Book of births of the Parish of [St. Bernard] in the place
of [Salina] frazione

Year, month, day and hour of birth, and day the newborn was
presented for baptism Newborn Information Surname and
first name [male female]State of the person [Legitimate illegit-
imate] First name, surname and domicile of the motherSalina

1. Teresa Pedretti of the late William and the late Teresa
Cerletti was born February 19, 1840

2. Her sister, Catherine of the late William and Theresa
Cerletti was born November 14, 1843.

3. Her sister Maria of the late William and the late Teresa
Cerletti born January 17, 1845

4. Her brother Francis, of the late William and late Teresa Cerletti was born December 19, 1847, married in America

5. Her brother, William of the late William and late Teresa Cerletti was born April 8, 1825, Chili

6. Her brother Sylvester of the late William and late Teresa Cerletti was born on November 10, 1827 America died there on 4 December 1875 in America

7. Her brother Bernardo of the late William and late Teresa Cerletti was born on January 1, 1834 lives in Zurich with his wife

The Book of Births Tavola 74, Tabella 3
Birth dates of 11 of Guglielmo and Teresa Pedretti's 15 children
Updated about 1898

The Book of Births Tavola 74, Tabella 3
Birth dates of 11 of Guglielmo and Teresa Pedretti's 15 children
Updated about 1898

CHIESA di S.BERNARDO - Registro "Stato Delle Anime"

(scritto alla fine dell'ottocento circa, con aggiornamenti successivi)

Figliolanza completa di PEDRETTI Guglielmo e
CERLETTI Teresa

(n. 17.4.1804, + 1.12.1869 - n. 21.1.1805, + 29.1.1853,

nati e morti a S.Bernardo)

TAVOLA 16 - Tabella 4

" 74 - "

- 1- *GUGLIELMO (tav.16 ,tab.4) , n. 8.Aprile 1825, emigrato nell'America del Sud, Ghili, (in quale Stato ?)*

- 2 - STEFANO n. 15.8.1826, emigrò negli Stati Uniti, e lì è morto nell'Aprile 1869, sposò una donna di Locarno

(Svizzera - Canton Ticino) e lasciò cinque figli,

- 3 - SILVESTRO n. 10.11.1827, morto negli Stati Uniti, celibe,

- 4 - LORENZO n. 5.12.1828, sposò a S.Bernardo, Maria Anna Lombardini fu Tomaso, morì il 16.12 1870,

si ammogliò il 2.5.1865, ebbe due ragazze, morte ambedue,

- 5 - MARIANNA n. 10.8.1830, morta a S.Bernardo il 18.6.1831,

- 6 - MARIANNA n. 8.4.1832 a S.Bernardo e quì maritata il 16.12.1863 con De Stefani Giuseppe di Guglielmo,

di Olmo,(Paese vicino a S.Bernardo) dove ebbe il domicilio; morì il 28.5.1894,

- 7 - BERNARDO n. 1.1.1834 si sposò nel Canton Neuchtel (Svizzera) con una riformata (Protestante) ebbe

una figlia, morta in tenera età; morì a Pallanza (Italia, provincia
di Verbania)

il 15.3.1894,

- 8 - ANTONIO n. 16.1.1836, morto negli Stati Uniti nel luglio
del 1869; celibe,

- 9 - GUGLIELMO n. 5.4.1837 e morto lo stesso giorno a
S.Bernardo,

- 10 - MARGHERITA n. 2.7.1838, sposatasi con Giuseppe
Donarelli di Sommarovina (Comune di S,Giacomo Filippo) nel
1868 circa e morì nella stessa Parrocchia, circa il 1872,

- 11 - *TERESA (tab.16, tab,4) n .17.2.1840, morta il 2.11.1899,
nella casa di ricovero di Mese (vicino a Chiavenna),*

- 12 - MARIA ORSOLA n. 13.10.1841, sposò De Stefani Battista
di Sommarovina il ? ; morì indetta Parrocchia nel febbraio 1868
? ,

- 13 - *CATERINA (tav.16, tab.4) n. 14.11.1843, morta il 3 agosto
1922 a Sommarovina ,*

- 14 - *MARIA (tav. 16, tav.4) n. 17.1.1845, morta il 7 febbraio
1916 a S.Bernardo ,*

- 15 - FRANCESCO n. 19.12.1847 , maritato a ? (*) ,in America
del Sud e lì è morto il 9.12 1894,

(*) Località di difficile lettura, in quale Stato? Argentina,
Uruguay, ... ? S.Bernardo - ottobre 2009 - ac. Mf

The Book of Births Tavola 16, Tabella 3
Birth dates of 3 of Guglielmo and Teresa Pedretti's 15 children
Updated about 1922
Above is the right page giving full information.
Lower facsimile shows the two pages together

Provincia di Sondrio
Distretto di Chiavenna
Commune di S. Giacomo
   S. Bernardo Li 4 Settembre 1831

Faccio fede io sottoscritto, Che nel Registro
Parrocchiale Battesimale trovasi registrato
alla pagina 202 atto 1.° Guglielmo Antonio
Maria Pedretti figlio del fù Pietro, e della
fù Anna Pedretti conjugi di questa Parrocchia
di S. Bernardo, nato il giorno nove 9 Settem=
bre dell'anno 1798, e batezzato il detto
giorno. In fede &.   Francesco Antonio Coltesi
                     Curato —

Birth Certificate
Guglielmo Antonio Mara Pedretti
September 4, 1832

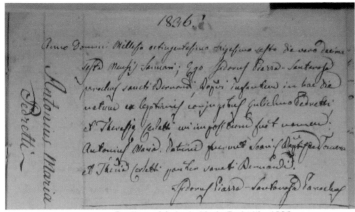

Baptism of Antonio Maria Pedretti - 1836

Baptism Record
Antonio Maria Pedretti
February 13, 1836

In the year of our Lord one thousand and eight hundred and thirty-six, on the thirteenth day of February, I, Isidoro Piazza Santarosa, parson of San Bernardo baptized the infant born today to the legitimate spouses Guglielmo Pedretti and Teresa Cerletti, who imposed the name Antonio Maria. The godparents were Giovanni Battista Tomera and Teresa Cerletti.

Isidoro Piazza Santarosa

Teresa Cerletti – died in 29 January 1853

Certificate of Death

Teresa Cerletti –Pedretti

January 29, 1853

In the Year of Our Lord, 1853, on the 29th day of January, Teresa Cerletti died at age 50. She was the wife of Guglielmo Pedretti. She was buried on the 30th day of the month in marked grave in San Bernardo cemetery.

Peter Crameri, Pastor

PASSENGER	AGE	SEX	OCCUPATION	PRVLS	DES		PASSENGER	AGE	SEX	OCCUPATION	PRVLS	DES
RUIZ, FREDERIC	26	M	FARMER	SR000	NY		ROSINE	42	F	FARMER	WM000	NY
LUOVIU, FREDERIC	28	M	FARMER	SR000	NY		FREDERIC	24	M	FARMER	WM000	NY
HOFFMANN, MARTIN	18	M	FARMER	SR000	NY		RHETHE	11	F	FARMER	WM000	NY
SCHMIDT, PETER	18	M	FARMER	SR000	NY		WILHELM	7	M	CHILD	WM000	NY
BURGHOLL, LEONHARD	54	M	FARMER	SR000	NY		CAROLINE	4	F	CHILD	WM000	NY
PIERRE	40	M	FARMER	SR000	NY		XACKER, JOH.CARL	18	M	FARMER	WM000	NY
MARGARITE	40	F	FARMER	SR000	NY		BLAICH, JOH.CARL	44	M	BOHR	WM000	NY
YORGENTA	7	F	CHILD	SR000	NY		CATHRINE	36	F	BOHR	WM000	NY
RRLIE	.09	M	INFANT	SR000	NY		PAULINE	14	F	BOHR	WM000	NY
HOFFMANN, ADAN	39	M	FARMER	PR000	NY		GOTTLIEB	12	M	BOHR	WM000	NY
RRINK, JAQUES	45	M	FARMER	PR000	NY		GOTTLOB	11	M	BOHR	WM000	NY
MARIA	47	F	FARMER	PR000	NY		LOUISE	9	F	CHILD	WM000	NY
MARIA	16	F	FARMER	PR000	NY		KURTZ, ODILIA	42	F	BOHR	WM000	NY
JEAN	10	M	FARMER	PR000	NY		FRIEDERICH	20	M	BOHR	WM000	NY
CATHRINE	8	F	CHILD	PR000	NY		OTHILIA	16	F	BOHR	WM000	NY
MATHIAS	30	M	FARMER	PR000	NY		EUPHROSINE	13	F	BOHR	WM000	NY
A.MARIA	42	F	FARMER	PR000	NY		EUGENIE	9	F	CHILD	WM000	NY
MARIA	26	F	FARMER	PR000	NY		FRENK, NICOLAS	29	M	FARMER	PR000	NY
KAEUFER, LAURENT	25	M	FARMER	PR000	NY		KILLY, GINDI	23	M	FARMER	BO000	NY
SOHRER, CATHRINE	25	F	FARMER	PR000	NY							
STEPHAN, JEAN	24	M	FARMER	PR000	NY							
DIEDIER, JEAN	34	M	FARMER	FR000	NY							
FENERSTEIN, XAVIER	32	M	FARMER	BO000	NY							
LEOPOLD	20	M	FARMER	BO000	NY							
WINGRELE, PAUL	52	M	FARMER	BO000	NY		SHIP:	CONNECTICUT				
PALLOSSIER, L.RUHGE	39	N	FARMER	FR000	NY							
STRAUS, ADOLPH	15	M	FARMER	BY000	NY		FROM:	HAVRE				
MEKETIER, AUGUSTE	32	M	BXR	FR000	NY		TO:	NEW YORK				
SONNENDENANN, MATHIAS	31	M	TLR	BO000	NY		ARRIVED:	23 AUGUST 1854				

p 103

PASSENGER	AGE	SEX	OCCUPATION	PRVLS	DES		PASSENGER	AGE	SEX	OCCUPATION	PRVLS	DES
PEDRETTI, HANS	27	M	FARMER	SR000	NY		SCHULTHESS, HEINRICH	27	M	FARMER	SR000	NY
REUEL, PETER	29	M	FARMER	SR000	NY		SONNISTER, FRANZ	22	M	FARMER	SR000	NY
LUTTO, LEONHARD	33	M	FARMER	SR000	NY		LEN, BALTH.	27	M	FARMER	SR000	NY
MARIE, J.JOS.	27	M	FARMER	SR000	NY		HOTTINGER, GREGOR.	22	M	FARMER	SR000	NY
ROSTETTER, ANDR.	38	M	FARMER	SR000	NY		MULLER, MAGDAL	21	F	FARMER	SR000	NY
ROPAT, JOS.	35	M	FARMER	SR000	NY		ARBER, HEINRICH.JB.	48	M	FARMER	SR000	NY
FIBRIAM, JOH.	26	M	FARMER	SR000	NY		ANNA	43	F	FARMER	SR000	NY
ROSIG, JACOB	22	M	FARMER	SR000	NY		HEINRI.CASP.	46	M	FARMER	SR000	NY
REULI, MATTI	16	M	FARMER	SR000	NY		CASPAR	24	M	FARMER	SR000	NY
RAVIZZA, JOSEPH	21	M	FARMER	SR000	NY		SAMUEL	22	M	FARMER	SR000	NY
DELLA, PIETRA-LUIGI	24	M	FARMER	SR000	NY		GOTTLIEB	18	M	FARMER	SR000	NY
ANTON	22	M	FARMER	SR000	NY		DAVID	17	M	FARMER	SR000	NY
RAVIZZA, LAURENZ	24	M	FARMER	SR000	NY		JOHANN	13	M	FARMER	SR000	NY
FRANKOLINI, ERASMUS	25	M	FARMER	SR000	NY		CARL	10	M	FARMER	SR000	NY
PAIAROLA, THOMAS	26	M	FARMER	SR000	NY		EDUARD	9	M	CHILD	SR000	NY
PEDRETTI, JOH.	27	M	FARMER	SR000	NY		A.ELISABETH	7	F	CHILD	SR000	NY
LOMBARDINI, THOMAS	59	M	FARMER	SR000	NY		ROSINE	2	F	CHILD	SR000	NY
PAIAROLA, PETER	34	M	FARMER	SR000	NY		LUEGGIER, A.MARIE	22	F	FARMER	SR000	NY
ANTON	28	M	FARMER	SR000	NY		CHRISTEN, JOS.MARIE	33	F	FARMER	SR000	NY
LOMBARDINI, THOMAS	50	M	FARMER	SR000	NY		FRANSISKA	28	F	FARMER	SR000	NY
GRISSMOTT, ANTON	50	M	FARMER	SR000	NY		DOROTHEA	23	F	FARMER	SR000	NY
ROSTETTER, GEORG	18	M	FARMER	SR000	NY		RIBLE, JOS.ANTH.	29	M	FARMER	SR000	NY
PIGNI, CATHARINA	32	F	FARMER	SR000	NY		SCHICK, AM.LOUISE	20	F	FARMER	SR000	NY
GRIGOTT, THOMAS	26	M	FARMER	SR000	NY		ZWALD, CASPAR	17	M	FARMER	SR000	NY
GREDIG, BARTHOL.	27	M	FARMER	SR000	NY		BARBARA	26	F	FARMER	SR000	NY
GELI, JOHANN	18	M	FARMER	SR000	NY		NAEGELI, CASPARD	24	M	FARMER	SR000	NY
MARK, CHRIST.	25	M	FARMER	SR000	NY		KREBS, JACOB	33	M	FARMER	SR000	NY
DOLF, JOHANN	34	M	FARMER	SR000	NY		SUSANNA	25	F	FARMER	SR000	NY
LORENZET, JOSEPH	28	M	FARMER	SR000	NY		MA.ELISE	.01	F	INFANT	SR000	NY
SUTTEN, BARTHOLOM	23	M	FARMER	SR000	NY		HAENNY, FRIEDR.	19	M	FARMER	SR000	NY
CORAY, JOHANN	20	M	FARMER	SR000	NY		CHRIST.	16	M	FARMER	SR000	NY
GUSTIN, JOHANN	20	M	FARMER	SR000	NY		LAENG, JOHANN	40	M	FARMER	SR000	NY
CRAVERS, JACOB	31	M	FARMER	SR000	NY		MARIA	35	F	FARMER	SR000	NY
FILIPPINO, IN.R.IPP	27	M	FARMER	SR000	NY		MARIA	12	F	FARMER	SR000	NY
PEDRETTI, WILHELM	29	M	FARMER	SR000	NY		JOHANNES	9	M	CHILD	SR000	NY
STEPHAN	28	M	FARMER	SR000	NY		FRIEDRICH	7	M	CHILD	SR000	NY
SILVESTRE	21	M	FARMER	SR000	NY		GOTTLIEB	5	M	CHILD	SR000	NY
DERUNDO, BLASIUS	28	M	FARMER	SR000	NY		RUDOLPH	.09	M	INFANT	SR000	NY
CAMENISCH, MARTIN	18	M	FARMER	SR000	NY		LANG, FRIEDRICH	25	M	FARMER	SR000	NY
CADIELI, JOHANN	25	M	FARMER	SR000	NY		MAURER, JOHANNES	50	M	FARMER	SR000	NY
PAIAROLA, ANTHON.	31	M	FARMER	SR000	NY		KAERLI, MELCHIOR	18	M	FARMER	SR000	NY
CAPROL, JOHANN	25	M	FARMER	SR000	NY		CATHARINA	17	F	FARMER	SR000	NY
LOMBARISEO, CASPAR	18	M	FARMER	SR000	NY		BERGER, MELCHIOR	32	M	FARMER	SR000	NY
BETERNI, JN.BAPTISTE	30	M	FARMER	SR000	NY		FRIEDERICH, ELISAB.	20	F	FARMER	SR000	NY
MUNGER, J.P.	30	M	FARMER	SR000	NY		MILLER, FRIEDR.	20	M	FARMER	SR000	NY
STIEFERHER, J.B.	30	M	FARMER	SR000	NY		MEYER, JOS.	28	M	FARMER	SR000	NY
BATIS, CHRISTIAN	23	M	FARMER	SR000	NY		JUNGMANN, FRIEDR.	50	M	FARMER	SR000	NY
HALI, PETER	27	M	FARMER	SR000	NY		WEBER, JOSEPH	28	M	FARMER	SR000	NY
HEHN, ANTON	46	M	FARMER	SR000	NY		STADLER, JOSEPH	40	M	FARMER	SR000	NY
CARDERINA, CHRISTIAN	30	M	FARMER	SR000	NY		STUDER, JOSEPH	50	M	FARMER	SR000	NY
EGGER, MICHEL	34	M	FARMER	SR000	NY		MA.JOSEPHINE	50	F	FARMER	SR000	NY
WAGCHLER, JOH.JOS.	36	M	FARMER	SR000	NY		AA.MARIA	27	F	FARMER	SR000	NY
MAGDALENA	35	F	FARMER	SR000	NY		NICOLAS	20	M	FARMER	SR000	NY
FR.ANTON	10	M	FARMER	SR000	NY		ROBERT	21	M	FARMER	SR000	NY
ELISE	8	F	CHILD	SR000	NY		WITHIER, JEANETTE	18	F	FARMER	SR000	NY
KERORO, CARL	30	M	FARMER	SR000	NY		MILLER, ANTON	31	M	FARMER	SR000	NY
GRBIM, JACOB	31	M	FARMER	SR000	NY		STUDER, JN.R.	47	M	FARMER	SR000	NY
							WENMEYER, MELCH.	34	M	FARMER	SR000	NY

Boat Manifesto for The Connecticut
William, Stephen and Sylvester Pedretti
August 23, 1854

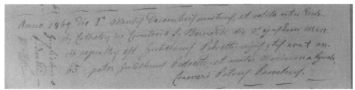

Guglielmo Maria Pedretti – died 1 December 1869

Certificate of Death
Guglielmo Maria Pedretti
December 1, 1869

The year was 1869 on the first day of December, he died. With the usual ritual of the Catholic Church, in the Cemetery of San Bernardo, on second day of the month the cited was buried Guglielmo Pedretti. His age was 65 years old. His father was Guglielmo Pedretti and his mother was Mariana Paiarola.

Peter Crameri – Pastor

Wedding Certificate, Stephen Pedretti & Adelaide Lombardi
6 Feb. 1858

State of Wisconsin, Bad Ax County

Be it remembered that on the twenty sixth day February A. D. 1858 in the town of Harmony, Mr. Stephen Pareta [Pedretti] of Badax City and Miss Adelaide Lombardi of Badax City were with their mutual consent legally joined together in Holy Matrimony which was solemnized by me in the presence of Fredric Guscetti of the town of Harmony and John Aurilla of the town of Harmony attending witnesses. Having been first satisfied by the oath of Mr. Stephan Pareta duly administered by me that there was no legal infringement to such marriage. ------ given under my hand at Badax City this the twenty-sixth day of February 1858. Namison Sayno, Director of the Peace

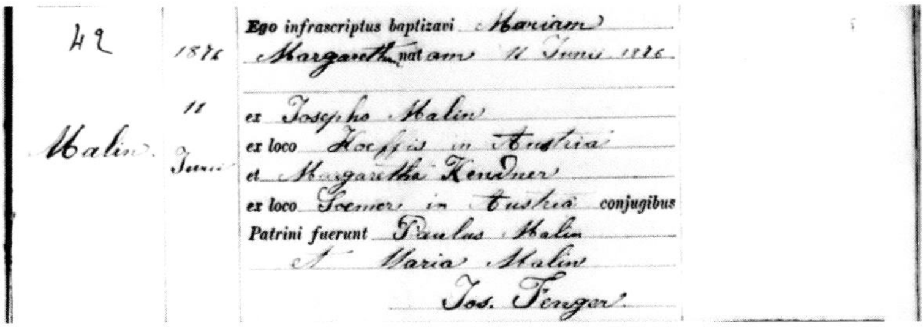

42 1876 11 Junii Malin

Ego infrascriptus baptizavi Mariam Margaretham natam 11 Junii 1876
ex Josepho Malin
ex loco Hoeffis in Austria
et Margaretha Kendner
ex loco Goemer in Austria conjugibus
Patrini fuerunt Paulus Malin
et Maria Malin
Jos. Fenger

Baptism Record Mary Margaret Malin, born 11 June 1876

	No. 187 33
1. Full name of husband	Peter Pedreth
2. Name of the father of husband	Stephen Pedreth
3. Name of the mother of husband before marriage	Adelaide Fombardi
4. Occupation of husband	Farmer
5. Residence of husband	Genoa Vernon Co.
6. Birthplace of husband	Ioa
7. Full name of wife previous to marriage	Mary Margaret Malin
8. Name of the father of wife	Joseph Malin
9. Name of the mother of wife before marriage	Margaret Guntnor
10. Birthplace of wife	Pittsburg Pennsylvania
11. Time when the marriage was contracted	November 26 1895
12. The place, town or township, and county, where the marriage was contracted	Genoa Vernon Co. Wis
13. The color of the parties	White
14. By what ceremony contracted	Catholic
15. Names of subscribing witnesses	Stephan Pedreth and Mary Malin
16. Name of person pronouncing marriage	Henry J Wirtz
17. Residence of person last named	Genoa Vernon Co. Wis
18. Date of certificate or affidavit of marriage	Dec 4 1895
19. Date of registration	Dec 6 1895
20. Any additional circumstances	Got dispensation from the Bishop

*Wedding Certificate Peter Pedretti and Mary Margaret Malin – 4
December 1895*

Certificate of Death – Adelaide Lombardi Pedretti –
10 Feb. 1911

P 3   LA CROSSE TRIBUNE   TUESDAY, AUGUST 11, 1914

COMRADES UNABLE
TO SWIM---DROWNS

Only Member of Party Who
Can Swim Goes Down
with Friends
Near-by

With men within a stone's throw who could not swim, Joseph Pedretti, 16 year old son of a prominent Italian farmer living east of Genoa, met death Sunday afternoon in a deep slough off the Mississippi river. Pedretti went to the slough with others. They could not swim. He donned a bathing suit and had been in the water several minutes. At the time he went under, he had swum across the slough and was returning, say those with him.

He made half of the distance returning when he sank. He did not call for help. The men told the boy's parents that they would have lost their lives had they tried to save him.

It was but a short time when help was summoned, a small drag was used and the boy's body brought to the shore.

Seven brothers and two sisters besides his father and mother survive Pedretti.

Funeral services were held this morning at the Catholic church at Genoa.

Joseph Pedretti drowns in Mississippi -- 9 August 1914
COMRADES UNABLE
TO SWIM---DROWNS

Only Member of Party Who
Can Swim Goes down
with Friends
Near-by

- - - -

With men within a stone's throw who could not swim, Joseph Pedretti, 16 year old son of a prominent Italian farmer living east of Genoa, met death Sunday afternoon in a deep slough off the Mississippi River.

Pedretti went to the slough with others. They could not swim. He donned a swimming suit and had been in the water several minutes. At the time he went under, he had swam across the slough and was returning, say those with him.

He made half of the distance returning when he sank. He did not call for help. The men told the boy's parents that they would have lost their lives had they tried to save him.

It was but a short time when help was summoned, a small drag was used and the boy's body brought to the shore.

Seven brothers and two sisters besides his father and mother survive Pedretti.

Copy of Death Record – Margaret Malin- Pedretti –
14 Sept 1921

MRS. MARGERET PEDRETTI

Mrs. Margeret Pedretti, wife of Mr. Peter Pedretti, living two miles east of Genoa, died Wednesday at 2 p. m. at her home. Mrs. Pedretti, whose maiden name was Malin, was born at Pittsburgh, Pa., June 11, 1876. She was married to Mr. Pedretti at Genoa 26 years ago. She is survived by her husband, seven sons and three daughters and her mother, Mrs. Malin of Genoa. The funeral will be held Saturday from the home at 8 a. m. and from the St. Charles Catholic church at Genoa at 9 o'clock. Rt. Rev. A. Ph. Kramer will officiate. Burial will be made at the Genoa Catholic cemetery.

Page 6   **La Crosse Tribune and Leader-Press**   **Friday September 16**

1921

Obituary

Mrs. Margaret Pedretti, wife of Mr. Peter Pedretti, living two miles east of Genoa, died Wednesday at 2 p. m. at her home. Mrs. Pedretti, whose maiden name was Malin, was born at Pittsburgh, Pa. June 11, 1876. She was married to Mr. Pedretti at Genoa 26 years ago. She is survived by her husband, seven sons and three daughters and her mother, Mrs. Malin of Genoa. The funeral will be held Saturday from the home at 8 a.m. and from the St. Charles Catholic church at Genoa at 9 o'clock. Rt. Rev. A. Ph. Kramer will officiate. Burial will be made at the Genoa Catholic Cemetery.

Obituary for Margaret Malin – died 14 September 1921

486

WISCONSIN STATE BOARD OF HEALTH
CERTIFICATE OF DEATH

Form No. VS 13-3-51-75M
State Birth No.

Local Registrar's No.

1. PLACE OF DEATH		2. USUAL RESIDENCE (Where deceased lived. If institution: residence before admission).	
a. COUNTY Vernon		a. STATE Wisconsin	b. COUNTY Vernon
b. CITY (If outside corporate limits, write RURAL and give) OR TOWN Vernon township)	c. LENGTH OF STAY (in this place) Life	c. CITY (If outside corporate limits, write RURAL and give township) OR TOWN Genoa	
d. FULL NAME OF HOSPITAL OR INSTITUTION (If not in hospital or institution, give street address or location) At Home		d. STREET ADDRESS (If rural, give location) R.F.D. #1	

3. NAME OF DECEASED (Type or Print)	a. (First) Peter	b. (Middle) Pedretti	c. (Last) Sr.	4. DATE OF DEATH (Month) 12 (Day) 14 (Year) 51

5. SEX Male	6. COLOR OR RACE White	7. MARRIED, NEVER MARRIED, WIDOWED, DIVORCED (Specify) Widower	8. DATE OF BIRTH 1/25/1861	9. AGE (In years) 90	If under 1 year Months 10 Days	If under 24 hrs. Hours Min.

10a. USUAL OCCUPATION (Give kind of work done during most of working life, even if retired) Retired	10b. KIND OF BUSINESS OR INDUSTRY	11. BIRTHPLACE (State or foreign country) Genoa, Wisconsin	12. CITIZEN of WHAT COUNTRY U.S.A.

13. FATHER'S NAME Stephen Pedrette	14. MOTHER'S MAIDEN NAME N. K.

15. WAS DECEASED EVER IN U.S. ARMED FORCES? (Yes, no or unknown) (If yes, give war or dates of service) X	16. SOCIAL SECURITY NO. X	17. INFORMANT Stephan Pedrette

18. CAUSE OF DEATH Enter only one cause per line for (a), (b), and (c)	MEDICAL CERTIFICATION	Interval Between Onset and Death
*This does not mean the mode of dying, such heart failure, asthenia, etc. It means the disease, injury, or complication which caused death.	I. DISEASE OR CONDITION DIRECTLY LEADING TO DEATH*(a) Chronic Myocarditis	
	ANTECEDENT CAUSES Morbid conditions, if any, giving rise to the above cause (a) stating the underlying cause last. DUE TO (b) Senility	
	DUE TO (c)	
	II. OTHER SIGNIFICANT CONDITIONS Conditions contributing to the death but not related to the disease or condition causing death.	

UNCERTIFIED COPY
NOT VALID
FOR IDENTITY PURPOSES

19a. DATE OF OPERATION	19b. MAJOR FINDINGS OF OPERATION	20. AUTOPSY? Yes ☐ NO ☐

21a. ACCIDENT SUICIDE HOMICIDE (Specify)	21b. PLACE OF INJURY (e.g., in or about home, farm, factory, street, office bldg., etc.)	21c. (CITY, TOWN, OR TOWNSHIP)	(COUNTY)	(STATE)
21d. TIME OF INJURY (Month) (Day) (Year) (Hour) m.	21a. INJURY OCCURRED While at Work ☐ Not While At Work ☐	21f. HOW DID INJURY OCCUR?		

22. I hereby certify that I attended the deceased from 19 4 to July 19 51 that I last saw the deceased alive on July 19 51 and that death occurred at m., from the cause and on the date stated above.

22a. SIGNATURE D. F. Doyle M.D.	(Degree or title)	22b. ADDRESS La Crosse, Wis.	22c. DATE SIGNED 12/17/51

24a. BURIAL, CREMATION, REMOVAL (Specify) Burial	24b. DATE 12/18/51	24c. NAME OF CEMETERY OR CREMATORY St. Charles	24d. LOCATION (City, town or county) Genoa, Wisconsin	(State)

DATE REC'D BY LOCAL 12-22-1951	REGISTRAR'S SIGNATURE Wm. Kotvis	25. FUNERAL DIRECTOR Paul J. Morris	ADDRESS

Certificate of Death – Peter Pedretti 14 December 1951

Pedretti Family Crest found in museum
in Campodolcino

The Sanctuary of Gallivaggio – Where many Vener and Starlochi ancestors were married

The home of the last Pedretti to live in San Bernardo, Sondrio, Italy

The Heroic Epic: an Essay

"I sing of arms and man"

-Virgil, *The Aeneid*

"I sing of kindness and woman"

-Pedretti, *The Story of Our Stories*

It is the spring of 1960 and our senior class has just completed reading Virgil's *The Aeneid* in Latin. Our professor, James Coke, who has walked us through Virgil's insights with love and kindness, opens the dialogue to discuss other epics and their influence on the peoples for whom they were written. He cites among others the *Iliad* and the *Odyssey*, the *Bible*, *Beowulf*, *The Divine Comedy*, *Paradise Lost*, *Mahabharata*, and *Epic of Gilgamesh*. Each portrayed heroes and/or creatures of otherly worlds, larger than life but also deeply flawed, who took on "evil forces" in a multifarious but structured manner that became the common memory of the peoples for whom they spoke. The epics forged for their society a new paradigm that set ethical standards, established limitations that curbed natural freedoms, and loomed with subliminal power over the consciousness of generations to come as the power of their words and stories foreshadowed, predicted and triggered events to come. All celebrated the warrior, war, violence, revenge [sometimes disguised as justice], and the ultimate victory of might and the establishment of a privileged class. [These thoughts may more reflect the thinking of an impressionable student than the words of the professor].

Coke states dogmatically, "No nation can come into its own without its own epic." Then with arrogance, which is quite unlike Professor Coke, he states, leaving little room for discussion, "America will never have an epic as we have no heroes of epic magnitude; we fought no wars that shaped who we are; we have no Junos we believe we can thwart, no enemy worthy of their own epic if they had defeated us. Let's look again at Virgil's opening lines." He reads them aloud to us:

Arma virumque cano, Troiae qui primus ab oris Italiam, fato profugus, Laviniaque venit litora, multum ille et terris iactatus et alto vi superum saevae memorem Iunonis ob iram; multa quoque et bello passus, dum conderet urbem, inferretque deos Latio, genus unde Latinum, Albanique patres, atque altae moenia Roma

Musa, mihi causas memora, quo numine laeso, quidve dolens, regina deum tot volvere casus insignem pietate virum, tot adire labores impulerit. Tantaene animis caelestibus irae?

[I will translate for you]
I sing of arms and of man, first in Italy
Birthed in Troy, he suffered in war, exiled by fate,
Cast out a vagabond, he braved the storms on land
        and sea
On account of the mindful wrath of Juno;

Until he came to the shores of Lavina,
Built a city to bring his gods to the Latin genus,
Fathered Alba Longa and the high walls of Rome.
Muse, remind me the grounds the queen god
Felt her power so injured, sensed ongoing disaster,
That pressed her to push this pious man
        through colossal
Trials. Is this the conduct of a heavenly god?
[Translation by author]

Coke continues, "What American poet could begin with those lines. None." Discussion over.

I think to myself, why does the great American Epic have to be about warriors and war? Why does today's epic have to be about limiting freedom? The epics of old met the needs of their society. Coke is, or at least should be right; we will never have that kind of epic.

"I sing of arms and of man." "I celebrate war and the warrior" is an equally good translation. The warrior in this case is Aeneas and the wars are the bloody battles that allow the Trojan refugee to eventually dominate the native Latins, take the capital city of Rome and began the long road of violence and aggression that established the Roman Empire.

Virgil is celebrating war and the bloodletting that comes with war. The hero is male, violent, flawed, victorious, vengeful, larger than life, who lives above the codes that the epic prescribes for the society who in the end is to be submissive to the hero and his offspring [in this case Augustus] who are also expected to discount every moral code that defines the society they lead. Does Aeneas mature into a more civilized being? Do his descendants? When does Virgil call for empathy, fairness or gentleness?

Virgil's epic ends in the cold-blooded revenge-murder of Turnus perpetrated by Aeneas, the "man" being sung about in the epic, just after he is victorious in taking Rome. He stands over his enemy and considers being compassionate, but when he sees Turnus wearing the belt of Pallas whom Turnus had slain in battle; Aeneas thrusts his sword "deep into his bosom." Virgil's epic ends in the "streaming blood" of the enemy and the glorious victory of arms and man:

> Aeneas volvens oculos dextramque repressit;
> et iam iamque magis cunctantem flectere sermo
> coeperat, infelix umero cum apparuit alto
> balteus et notis fulserunt cingula bullis
> Pallantis pueri, victum quem vulnere Turnus
> straverat atque umeris inimicum insigne gerebat.
> ille, oculis postquam saevi monimenta doloris
> exuviasque hausit, furiis accensus et ira
> terribilis: 'tune hinc spoliis indute meorum
> eripiare mihi? Pallas te hoc vulnere, Pallas
> immolat et poenam scelerato ex sanguine sumit.'
> hoc dicens ferrum adverso sub pectore condit
> fervidus; ast illi solvuntur frigore membra
> vitaque cum gemitu fugit indignata sub umbras.

> Translation by John Dryden
> And, just prepar'd to strike, repress'd his hand.
> He roll'd his eyes, and ev'ry moment felt
> His manly soul with more compassion melt;
> When, casting down a casual glance, he spied

The golden belt that glitter'd on his side,
The fatal spoils which haughty Turnus tore
From dying Pallas, and in triumph wore.
Then, rous'd anew to wrath, he loudly cries
(Flames, while he spoke, came flashing from his eyes)
"Traitor, dost thou, dost thou to grace pretend,
Clad, as thou art, in trophies of my friend?
To his sad soul a grateful off'ring go!
'T is Pallas, Pallas gives this deadly blow."
He rais'd his arm aloft, and, at the word,
Deep in his bosom drove the shining sword.
The streaming blood distain'd his arms around,
And the disdainful soul came rushing thro' the wound.

We see the proud and victorious Aeneas, the invader from Troy, stand over Turnus, the leader of the native Latins. Aeneas could have and almost does show compassion and spare the life of the defeated and humiliated Turnus. But revenge rules the day. When Aeneas sees that Turnus is wearing the armor of Aeneas' protégé Pallas, Aeneas raises his sword and thrusts it into Turnus killing him instantly and spilling his blood and soul on the ground to fertilize centuries of brutality and power known ironically as Pax Romana. The work concludes celebrating revenge, one of human's least honorable traits.

Was Coke right? Is there is no American "hero" that could measure up to the standards of heroism, violence and revenge established by Homer and Virgil?

Washington might seem a natural; but American puritanical mythology has turned him into goody-two-shoes far too frail for a major flaw considered a requirement for a classical epic hero. Probably impossible for an author to be able to change his reputation of a reluctant leader into a powerful [and far more honest] representation of the power-grabbing egocentric driven man that he was. Lincoln too has been immortalized on hallow grounds much too sacred for an epic hero. Plus he was far from a military hero. Whitman might do, but unlikely Americans would ever take a poet seriously enough, and he was the antithesis of the requisite warrior that Coke and others seemed to think was part and parcel of epic heroism. The idea of Jackson, Harrison, Grant, MacArthur, or Eisenhower serving as an epic hero parallel to Aeneas or Ulysses is too funny to even discuss. Benedict Arnold turned traitor. Teddy Roosevelt had the flaws but his victory was inconsequential. Lee and Jackson lost. Patton was too mean in more than one meaning of that word. In addition, few modern readers could be sucked into believing that supernatural heroes existed let alone had some power to impose on the choices we make. Hopefully, today's reader would not revel in cold blooded murder by a sheriff-judge-jury-and-executioner hero of the classical epic.

Still, it seemed to a young romantic, that there was something dead wrong in Coke's proclamation. Most obviously, if a nation could not come of age without an epic to support its perception of itself, and America could never have an epic; it meant America would never come of age – that seemed an odd prediction for a country that was destined to dominate world politics for generations to come. True, a country that had just elected baby-face JFK and lived through the years of Eisenhower apathy and naiveté, looked like it might never reach adolescent let alone develop a working cultural identity.

Still, most predicted world dominance and a short adolescence. [Only 50 years later, the election of a black president and the nomination of a woman for president could symbolize America is emerging into adulthood as a nation].

I asked myself, "Does an epic have to celebrate dominance, war and revenge? Why did an epic have to promote limitation, exclusion and restriction? Is it not possible to put the historic gentry sponsored classism, war, violence, and tribalism into the past? Wasn't the American hero the commoner, making things happen by mass commitment rather than individual supremacy? More willing to fight for fair treatment with words than domination by war? More concerned with kindness than control? Capable of letting empathy replace revenge? True, these traits of the American psyche had been obfuscated by writers and songsters, politicians and economists supported by clergy and educators who were still letting the idea of the plutocratic way of life seduce them into believing it was the only paradigm of progress.

Wasn't the mandate for a great epic the call to identify and celebrate who the people are and what their potential is? The Great American Epic will not honor militaristic chauvinist war-mongers that the press and politicians love, but the story of a gentle people, a benevolent people, who believe in the value of all humans and the necessity of fairness to rule supreme. True we are still a young people and easily duped; prey to the privileged propaganda. We almost always substitute revenge for justice; justice for equality and equality for fairness; we naively have been convinced we can do good with arms when we know that fairness and impartial concern is the order of the day. Yes, we continue to seek heroes by super-imposing "heroism" on men who play silly but violent sports games, fight illegal wars, and on photogenic faces that make it to the big screen, but deep down we know that the hero in our culture is our neighbor and her family. While we, from time to time, idolize the woman next door, we are still not convinced that she holds the present and the future in her hands, that she is who we are, that she represents what we can become far more than Reagan, Bush, Clinton, or Obama; a zillion times more than O.J., A-Rod, Dr. J, Liberace, Madonna, Mr. T or Oprah. We know, even as we worship them, that it is the verity made in their image that is the big lie; that it is what continues to keep us in our place, distracts us from both reaching beyond our self-imposed limitations and from finding in ourselves the power to transform, to leave war and violence behind us, to forge a future free of nationalism, religion and weapons of destruction. We have the wherewithal to drive starvation, violence, murder, war, crimes against humanity to relics of the past; let them join human sacrifice, slavery and medieval torture as inconceivable practices once proudly perpetrated by humans on humans. If a national epic can bring a people to their potential, the real but hidden America was crying out for that epic to be written. And maybe, just maybe, the task was mine.

For fifty years that challenge stayed with me; alive, nibbling at my heart and soul and from time to time my brain. Along the way I had some realizations. The American epic hero would be a planter – one who planted and cultivated. Our hero had no power or desire to steal the work of others. This insight was followed by an awareness that our hero could not come from the privileged class, by definition a people who rely on other's plantings. Our story was not the story - could not be the story - of someone indulging in the unjust wealth born of other's labor.

As I traveled through life and the world over, I kept an eye out for that hero but did not find him – wondered in fact if he even existed; for a long time I thought Whitman was the rightful American epic hero; I also seriously considered my grandfather and Elvis. Three heroes for sure; but not the epic hero I needed to inspire and make a story. I tested Jeannette Rankin, but her story never sparked into a word; for a while I determined that Toni Morrison seemed a natural – a giant among humans, a great woman, the archetypal American success, but it was not the American dream that would provide the skeleton for our epic. In a prequel, my mother was a promising candidate. I got a novel out of her life story – but not an epic by any definition. There was a clown that seemed right. She seemed perfect, and I found the idea of a clown hero full of potential. I could not find the first word to start the story for I could not overcome my biased predisposition that I would have to defend for you that clown hero was inherently right. To defend is to discredit.

Only when I stopped looking, did I find that the model for our epic hero had always been in my own backyard – a place that appeared to be an isolated little community of self-sufficient partisans who appeared to know of love only how to withhold it and of hope only that it was for the next life. Their faith was deep but had no breadth; it was a faith in Jesus and what they believed to be his church. They rarely demonstrated anything except the local party line. At best they planted seeds on their farms, nourished them into growing, providing sustenance for many more. At worst, they seemed myopic and parochial. But as the saying goes, appearances can be deceiving.

When I was 5 or 6 years old, I could see that my grandfather Peter Pedretti was a man wise well beyond his 88 years. As I said, at one point I thought he might be the prototype for my epic hero. But he seemed more the exception than the exemplar.

I also sensed a force hovering around, under, over and inside the people who called home the bluffs and coulees along the east side of the Mississippi River just a few miles north of the place some had decided earlier would divide Minnesota from Iowa. I attributed that gut feeling to some false chauvinism about where I was raised. Don't we all think there is both something special and something disparaging about the place we called home in our formative years?

I knew little about these people, where they came from and why they populated this tiny spot which seemed a great distance even from the middle of nowhere. I visited late in the end of the last century and discovered a gentle people, a caring people. While pausing for a moment to admire a quality I had not known I had left behind, one of my double first cousins interrupts me to ask me if I know that Jim and Jean and a few others had undug a rich history of the two families that merged in the second quarter of the 20th century to produce 37 [more if you count those stillborn or who died within days of birth] members of my generation who share the same four grandparents [makes us more siblings than cousins]. At first, family curiosity piqued my interest. Soon I was deep into the search for more detail, more generations of ancestors, more insight into what made us who we are.

While returning from my first trip to the ancestral grounds of my family, I realized that the great American hero I had been searching for half a century to serve as the basis for my determination to write the great American epic was this family. The hero had been too close [my family] and too far away [family instead of individual] for me to see. Our epic would be about us, you and me. The characters would be our mother and our father, their parents and the parents of their parents. I say our, instead of my, because our mothers have always been the planter, the nourisher, the seeker of kindness. It is she that planted seeds, nourished the growth and fed humanity spiritually, mentally and corporeally. No matter if the seed was the germ of a plant, an idea, a creative impulse or scientific discovery; our mothers planted the seed in rich fertile soil, cultivated, fed and mothered it into nourishment for others. They never were serfs, never slave –owners, never hoarders, never violent, never war-mongers, never greed-worshippers or witch hunters. They were kind, empathic and generous. There when needed and never there when a bother. It was they, not the landed gentry of Virginia nor the elite Bostonians who were America. It is they, not the czars of corporate America nor the weasels of Wall Street who are America. It is they, not the lecturers of Ivy League nor the wily of Washington, who are America. It is they that are the future world citizen.

Their story is your story. Their story is the story of every human on earth who dreams of and struggles for freedom, forbearance and fairness. Their story is the story of every planter of seeds that was ever born; the planter of tomato seeds; of lilac roots, of idea seeds, of creation seeds, of discovery seeds, of fantasy seeds, of day dreamer seeds. Their story is not only the American Epic; their story is the story of the Great World Epic.

They know that first they must ask and each of us must ask afresh, "What does it mean to be human?" Without that question, "What does it mean to be American? Female? Jew? Black? Lutheran? Straight?" are simple absurdities.

The Story of Our Stories, filled with many stories, is one story – the story of champions as ingrained in kindness, empathy, generosity and life as those warrior heroes of past epics were ingrained in force, appetite, war and death. We celebrate the fruit of the planters of seeds; our precursors celebrated the demolition of bearers of arms.

My friend, you and I are no more prepared to worship war mongers than we are to look up to the gods of Olympia who constantly badgered the heroes of the warrior day. Come with me; listen to the story of our story, the stories of you and me, of our parents, their parents and their parents and grandparents, of our children and their children and their grandchildren. It is our story of planters, nurturers of advance, and tillers of nutrition, fairness and inspiration. It is our epic and it will haunt us until we sack the wagers of war, the supporters of starvation, the manufacturers of munitions, the bigots of nation-states, and the advocates of Abrahamism who prefer killing to devotion, doctrine to freedom and authority to fairness.

Come, join me in play, kindness and song.

I sing of kindness and of woman, first in life
Birthed in the Valley of St. James, always humbled
Ceaselessly derided, she sailed to the Land of the Turtle

Afflicted by the relentless fury of the great
    god Misogyny
Until she lay bare the Valley of Gentleness
Mothered empathy and the moat of gentleness sur-
    rounding harmony.
Muse, remind me of the grounds the sons
Felt their power so tattered, sensed terminal disaster,
That pressed them to push our mother through colossal
Trials. Is this the conduct of men of courage?
I sing of kindness and of woman
Who long since left the shores
Of craving, supremacy and war
To explore generosity, affection and creativity,
And of the suffering they endured
Trodden under the might of the Sons of Misogyny
Those ministers of misery who maltreated our mothers
Turning brother against sister, husband against wife,
Parent against child, mother against mother.
Tell me, reader, how it all began, why so much spite?
What did our mothers do to deserve their vengeance?
Priests indulging souls for tolls; peddling passports
    to heaven,
Soldiers raping for safekeeping they never sought,
Lords deflowering virgins by the bushel,
Gods unable or unwilling to speak.
Deceived, molested, ravished, ignored, pillaged
Our mother would not be ground into retaliation.
A Gentle Race, Fertile Mothers,
Serfs no more, never Lords
Planting wistful prairies of sustenance

Spiriting West to teeming land nourished for
A thousand years by the sons and daughters of
 the Turtle.
She spoke, "Poet, why are you silent?
Write the words
For you have what it takes
You have heard the stories
Of your mothers and all await your verses.
Sing in clarity; listen to the mothers:
'Starvation is as necessary as the King of France
Craving as dear as Ubu Roi
Supremacy as acceptable as the Tsar of Russia
Self-righteousness as tenable as the world is flat
Arrogance as useful as the British aristocracy
Let war and murder be impossible
As human sacrifice and Holokautein is impossible,
Let Jihad join witch hunting,
Revolution become unfashionable,
Nationalism writhe in its own provincialism,
Weapons join the woolly mammoth.
Come reader, join our mothers;
Seek joy, playfulness and love,
Reject servitude,
Abandon violence
For kindness is possible as you are possible

SYNOPSIS OF

THE STORY OF OUR STORIES

By pedretti

The Story of our Stories is the story of Peter and John, Adelaide and Stefano, Maria Prima, Maria Therese and Agnes and her children. It is the story of the individuals who peopled the Mount of San Bernardo and the Valley of Saint James who turned the roughness of Bad Ax into the gentleness of Genoa - but first and foremost it is our story, the story of you and me. Our story is written as an epic composed of 12 books each with a supportive addendum. Each book covers a different measurement, some covering the life of a typical family member of a specific generation, others reflecting many people of a generation, another tracing the entire story from beginning to now and one looking into a future predicated by the behavior of our mothers. Each volume tells a critical part of the story, is an integral part of the whole and plays into the unfolding of the epic. While arranged by number, each book can be read independent of the rest.

Abstract of twelve books

I. **Time to Journey Home,** A travelogue about my trip back to the homeland and how I was inspired to write *The Story of Our Stories*. The Addendum includes pre-1909 ahnentafel record of author, autobiographies of select persons who researched ancestry of family, a pictorial graphic, meaning of the surnames of our main characters, and a paper on the power of stories in our life.

II.   **The Veneid,** an epic poem telling of journey into afterlife [ala Divine Comedy] where I meet many of my mothers who celebrate woman and kindness [ala the Aeneid's celebration of man and war]. The addendum will trace the ahnentafel chart of the mothers; provide a chronology of major events, and an essay pondering the ultimate question.

III.   **Begetters of Children,** an historical fiction account of how the Pedretti family settled on San Bernardo Mountain, developed a village, farmed unfarmable land, avoided plagues, wars and other human disasters, had many children, immigrated to Genoa, Wisconsin, developed the land and populated half of America [I joke only a little here]. The addendum includes musings on the role of epic literature to shape human perspective, the ahnentafel story of Stefano Pedretti, facsimiles of vital records of San Bernardo, the story of our people's life on the mountainside accompanied with the historical evolution a republic government in Val San Giacomo.

IV.   **Lost Book of Maria Prima Della Morte an** adaptation of the journal maintained by Giovanni Vener about the life and accomplishments of his grandmother Maria Prima Della Morte. [1758-1817]. The Addendum will include the ahnentafel table of Giovanni Vener [DOB 13 March 1829], The story of Campodolcino – Val San Giacomo, primary documents showing vital information of Giovanni's ancestors and a treatise ascertaining the occurrence of trinity in everything.

V.   **L'ultima Preghiera** The last <u>prayer</u> of Marie Teresa Cerletti spoken aloud a day or two before her death on January 29, 1853 as she realizes that her Maker has called her too early to raise her family and to prevent her elder sons from abandoning their heritage to the dream of a better future. The addendum will include the Geno outline of the female linage going back to Eve, the stories of the major churches of worship where baptisms, marriages and funerals of our characters took place, and an article catechizing the god story.

VI.   **Lettere d'Amore** A score of <u>letters</u> written by Stefano Pedretti and Adelaide Lombardy as they court each other at great distances in 1853-1854. The last letter is written by Adelaide 40 years after she tragically lost the love of her life to a freak lumber accident.The addendum includes the ahnentafel chart of Adaelaide Lombardi tracing her family back to Airolo, Switzerland, the story of Airolo, primary documents of Adelaide's ancestry, an essay identifying the three stages of love and observations on the failure of compromise to resolve anything.

VII.   **John** Selections from the <u>diary</u> of a pioneer written while incarcerated in the Vernon County Insane Asylum at the turn of the century. John Venner spent the last days of his life confined and the diary fluctuates between manic days and depressed days. You get to see the inside of the head of an immigrant reliving the high points and the low points of being an innovator on the frontier. The addendum includes the ahnentafel listings of Giovanni's wife Mary Madeline Starlochi, the story of Genoa, primary documents found during research of Starlochi family, and a manifesto inspired by Giovanni calling for the end of war and starvation.

VIII.   **Peter** The <u>biography</u> of a transitional figure who dominates his community as the world leaves the age of horse and buggy for petro powered mass transportation. Peter Pedretti was the wisest man I ever met. He raised eleven children, mostly by himself as his wife died shortly after the birth of their youngest daughter. The addendum includes the ahnentafel listing of Peter's wife Maggie Malin, the story of Gofis and Eger home of the Malins and Petlarn the Bohemian home of Maggie's mother, pictures of family gravestones, an essay by Peter offering a path to making an ethical life and Peter's tract calling for a maximum [as opposed to minimum] wage.

IX.   **The Book of Agnes,** Selections from a <u>novel</u> about one of John's granddaughters, Agnes. It is a tale of the extraordinary life of one woman's gentle manner, kindness, and fertility over forty summers and forty winters, when capitalists' greed undermined the economic stability of the world, a deranged ethnic population inspired by a maniac caused the death of fifty million people and Soviet panic all but knocked out any remaining American sense and led to numerous wrongful wars. Walt Whitman had Agnes in mind when he eulogized her as one of the "numberless unknown heroes equal to the greatest heroes known." The addendum includes a list of Agnes' descendants, the ahnentafel chart of Agnes' mother Mary Caroline Nicolatti, the story of Trento and Trentino – the homeland of the Nichelati family, thoughts on the illogicality of classism and an essay on the need to put X back in Christmas.

X.   **Hoe-ers; Twelve Stories by Twelve Siblings**, the autobiographies of twelve of Agnes' 15 children accompanied by the "fake" dairies of two others. You will often read about the same event(s) told from different perspectives. The addendum will include the story of the 40 double cousins born grandchildren of both Peter Pedretti and Tom Venner along with the Geno story tracing their father's roots back to Northern Europe, the middle east, Africa and ultimately to Adam. The essay in this book will demonstrate that our worship of work - "get a job" - is nothing more than the continuation of the entitled keeping indentured serfs at service to their avarice.

XI.   **Mick: Planter of Seeds** Selections from the author's <u>memoirs</u> selected to show how a farm boy became a college professor and went on to become an international arts festival impresario. The addendum will include the ahnentafel chart of our author covering upwards of 480 ancestors, a photo essay telling with pictures and words the story of the immigrants who played the central role of turning this story into an epic, and select primary documents from the International Festivals made by the author and a short thesis suggesting a radical reordering of representation in the US House of Representatives. The essay in this book will reveal the great inequality perpetrated by the social security act and offer a full-proof solution to equalize and perpetuate social security ad infinitum.

XII.   **Il Lavoro di Artisti** A collection of <u>art work</u> created by members of the family from the fifth generation. Their work exemplifies that this family made art instead of going to war to express their creative energy. The Addendum will include the story of the children of Peter Pedretti and Bartholomew "Tom" Venner, It will also include some fun facts about the families, an abridgment of the story of the universe and a follow-up manifesto by a great- grandchild of John calling for the end of nation-states, monotheism, and weapons of destruction, the primary agents of war for the past three thousand years.

N.B. All subject to change

BOOKS BY PEDRETTI

The Story of Our Stories [12 volumes]

Delighting the Senses [2 volumes]

The Book of Agnes

27 poems on my left shoelace

Works in Progress

45

The Trinity

Fifty Questions

Little Book of Truths

The Truly Short History of Man

Mick: Memoirs of a Planter of Seeds